MW01492559

Copyright © 2015 Hitgalut Consultants

Cover design by:
Graphic Artist – Photographer, Nicholas Mukupa
and
Pathfinder http://www.pathfinder.smugmug.com

Forward

I thank my Father God who has made this book possible by stirring up the gifts and talents he has instilled in me.

I dedicate this book to all the individuals who have fought for freedom in their own country and for those who have died in the struggle of their independence.

I would like to thank my parents, Wilfred and Hope Chilangwa, who have supported me in all my works that I have endeavoured to achieve. I would also like to thank all my other family members and friends who have consistently stood with me and encouraged me to continue running the race of life.

Introduction

She slowly placed the receiver back onto its cradle and quietly sighed, almost feeling faint. Carefully, she carefully turned her tattered wristwatch band to look at the time. It was almost 6:30p.m. With her shoulders hung over in distress, she made her way to the coat hanger by the door and slipped on her coat and hat. Just as she was walking out the door, she caught her own reflection in the mirror by the front door and was caught by surprise by what she saw through the windows of her own heart. She trailed her fingertips along her dark complexion, feeling the waves and bumps of uncared for skin, which she always promised that one day, she would care for. She stared at herself for a moment and it finally occurred to her how old and tired she was feeling. Barely thirty-five, her thoughts that were filled with years of anxiety had layered her face with ten years of insinuating lines of fatigue. She touched herhair and fingered her chin and short neck. Saddened by her appearance, she couldn't help feeling ugly. Her hair was smoked with fine streaks of grey and the dark circles under her eyes were shadowed by the boulder bags of sleepless nights.

Her eyes had lost their youthful spark and glow of anticipation. She could not remember the last time she put make-up on or got her hair done at the salon. Her friends always told her that it was important to treat herself every now and then. She only mumbled that she had better use for her money. Now she knew what they

1

were talking about. She could see that they were politely telling her that she just wasn't looking right.

Her heart sunk to her feet, weighed down by thereality of how it seemed impossible for her to retrieve the lost years of her youth. She bit her lower lip and took a deep breath as she looked at her figure in the full-length mirror. She noticed how her full breasts were still looking firm and youthful. She still had her slim body looking erect and slender. An unexpected sense of confidence crept in to remind her that she still had her young smooth figure with extenuated curves of a fine black woman. This changed her perception of herself. She treasured that moment as she took in her fine figure. She turned from side to side and admired her angles and nothing else seemed ugly anymore. She was a beautiful sensual black woman with a sense of appeal and character.

With a sense of lightness in her heart, she sighed this time with confidence. She neatly tucked her uncombed hair underneath her hat and buttoned up her coat before walking out into the rain and down the street to the police station.

When she arrived at the station, she wondered what it was this time. In fact, it didn't matter what it was anymore, because it was going to be the last timehe was going to do this again. In her cool, yet shymanner, she entered the police station and thepoliceman behind the counter respectfully stood up to greet her.

"Hello, Mrs Bellmont." He said with a smallsmile, but yet couldn't help feeling sorry for her. Sheopened her mouth to answer, but she was swollenwith embarrassment. His pitying eyes fell on her andher voice was held back. She tried to divert her eyesfrom his when it just occurred to her that it was thethird time that month that she had come to thestation. She finally found her voice and said,

"I have come to pick up my boy."

To try and not make her feel bad, he changedhis pity to a look of reassurance. Regardless, she kepther eyes away from meeting his. He had seen andmet many women like Mrs Bellmont who weredescent mothers who had sons who kept getting intotrouble. He wondered what possessed their childrento go astray from heart-warming mothers like MrsBellmont.

"It's going to be all right, Mrs Bellmont." Hefinally reassured her. She nodded slightly and tried tofight back the tears with a forced widening smile.When they brought her son out, she frownedand narrowed her eyes at him like all the other times, but he rolled his eyes at her and walked on past herand out the door. He had seen her look a milliontimes and it did not seem to faze him any more thanit did the other times. What he did not know wasthat this time, he should have takenthat look moreseriously. She had plans for him now. Big plans.Without speaking to each other, they walked homethrough the London rain, he looking down at his feetand she was looking straight ahead of her. The moment they got home, he went straightupstairs to his room and she went to the kitchen toput the kettle on. Still wearing her raincoat, she satat the kitchen table and held her head in her hands.

She heard her son come down stairs and then pick upthe phone in the other room. She could hear himspeak briefly to one of his friends, but her thoughts inher head drowned his conversation. It was thepiercing whistling kettle that finally woke her andturned her thoughts into a throbbing templeheadache. She thought about turning off the piercingkettle that whistled endlessly in her ears, but she satat the table still holding her head in her hands lettingthe pain sink in and suppress her pain, fatigue andsense of loss. The throbbing headache swelled tearsup in her eyes.

"Mum, I'm going out." He announced from thekitchen door.

She did not hear him.

"Mum?" He called out to her again. When she didn't answer the second time, he walked into the kitchen and saw her sitting at the table with her head still in her hands. "Mum, are you okay?" He askedsounding a little worried. He knelt down beside herto try and see her face. She slowly lowered her handsfrom her face and with her puffy red eyes she finallylooked at him. "Mum?" He called her again. He could tell that in thought, she was still miles away. Her look was blinding and her face was starting to lookpasty.

"Turn off the kettle." she finally spoke. Matthew did as he was told and announced again to her, "I'm going out, mum." He waited a momentfor her to answer. She didn't turn around to look athim and they both looked at each other withoutsaying a word. He then turned and began to walkout."Matthew," she called out to him. While hewas in mid step, he turned around and answered,

"Yes, mum?"

"Sit down."

Matthew slowly walked across the smallkitchen and sat across from her at the kitchen table, acounter built into the wall.

"Help me, Matthew." Her voice cracked astears began to race down her face.

"What's wrong mum?" He became worried. She took a deep breath and said, "Help me understand why you do this tome,.....why you make me cry?"

4

Matthew didn't answer. He turned his eyesaway the moment he recognized the pain.

"I know that whatever I say won't make you stay home tonight...but just this once, I am begging you. Please, please stay home with your mama tonight." Without blinking, tears sailed down herflushed dark cheeks.

Oh, mum." He got up and put his arms around her and hugged her tight. "Please don't cry."

"My dear child, your mama is tired. I am tiredof you getting in trouble with the police, I am so tiredI just want to lie down and sleep and never wake up.But I can't. I stay up worrying about you and wonderwhether you are going to come home." "Oh mama, you know I would never leaveyou." He squeezed her tighter and felt that oldmothering feeling that he loved and knew so well. Heinhaled deeply and smelt that smell that alwayscomforted him and for a brief moment, he felt like hewas five again. He wanted to nestle up against herlarge soft bosom and be a child again.

"I want to die before you do." She said. He pulled away from her and was angry withher for saying that.

"Mama, don't talk like that. You are not goinganywhere and neither am I."

"Then stay home with your mama tonight."

"I just need to run out and get something."

"No."

"Mama,..."

"No." She interjected and narrowed her eyesat him. "What are you going to get? Some more drugs to sell in the streets? Or is it stolen moneyfrom that friend of yours?" Her tone changed withbitterness. "You bring shame to me and to the rest ofyour family."

"What family mama, what family! The onlyfamily I have is you."

5

"Don't forget your father."

"What father? I have no father. He left us along time ago. Didn't you always tell me that blood isthicker than water? Well, the man you call my fathersure as hell doesn't think so. As far as I amconcerned, I hope he rots in hell!"

She got up from her seat faster than they bothexpected and slapped him across the face.

"Now, you listen to me, boy. I won't have youtalking about your own blood like that. At least yourfather was not a liar or a cheat. He loved you and me. He did what he had to do."

"That's a right out lie mum, and you know it. I don't understand why you always defend him." Without straightening out his coat, he walked out of the house slamming the door behind him and almost making the mirror by the door fall.

She sat back down at the kitchen table aloneand cupped her face in her hands. She cried alone, mourned her God forsaken life alone, and prayed to God like she was the only soul left on the face of theearth. Forgetting about the water in the kettle forher tea, she went upstairs and went to bed.

In the middle of the night, a noise woke her. She opened her eyes wide in the dark and listenedcarefully. She heard the down stairs door close andshe heard someone come up the stairs. It was Matthew. She knew his steps too well. Relieved, sheclosed her eyes again and went back to sleep.

The next morning she went into his room andsat at the edge of his bed. She shook him and whenhe didn't respond, she shook him again and called outto him.

"Matthew, wake up." she said.

"What, mum." he rolled over to the other side and tried to pull the covers over his head. She pulled him back and ripped the covers off him.

"You come with me now. This nonsense is going to end. I want you to pack your bags right away. We are going away."

Her last words got his attention and he sat up.

"Where are we going?"

"Home."

"Wha....?"

"We are going home, Matthew." she picked up his clothes off the floor and threw them on his bed.

"I want you to pack your clothes, not your winter clothes, just your summer clothes. Where we are going, you won't need them." Still confused by what she was saying, Matthew looked at her and knew that he was not dreaming. She stopped, looked at him and with confidence said,

"Do as your mother tells you. A fifteen year old should not be questioning his mother's orders." With a suspicious smile, she turned around and walked out. In an hour, he had showered, changed and packed his bags. Just as he started his way down the stairs, he stopped and sat at the top of the stairs looking down at her. She eagerly looked out the window. She was wearing her best shoes that she only wore on Sundays. She was also wearing a brim hat and a little bit of make-up that she never wore.

He could not remember the last time his mother dressed so keenly. She nervously twisted her white hanky in her hands and walked a few steps to and from the window. She would look out the side window and then glance up at Matthew and then glance out the window again. Finally, the

7

excitementrose up in her and a broad smile grew on her face.

"The taxi's here." she finally said. Matthew still sat calmly at the top of the stairs.

"I am not going anywhere until you tell mewhere we are going."

"It's a surprise." She smiled nervously. Hedidn't move. He sat firmly on the stairs.

"Oh, alright...I promise to tell you once we get into the taxi." She continued to smile. Matthew thought for a moment and then grabbed his bag and met his mother at the bottom of the stairs. Before they got into the taxi, he helped her lock the front door securely and put their bags in the boot of the car.

"To the airport, please." She told the driver.

"Where are we going mum?"

"Home," She said smiling again. "We are going home."

On their quiet drive, Matthew leaned in close to her and asked her again,

"Where are we really going?"

"You'll see." She continued to smile and tried not to look nervous. They got to the airport and checked in at the counter and the lady politely asked her, "Are you checking your luggage all the way through Mrs Bellmont?"

"Yes. Yes, all the way."

"Will that be non-smoking or smoking?"

"Non-smoking.......please." She said to the pristine lady as she handed them back their tickets and their boarding passes. She gave them her trained customer service smile and said, "Have a nice flight."

"Thank you." She replied. Clenching onto the short handles of her little brown handbag with both hands, she walked down the long corridor following the signs to their gate. Matthew trailed behind her and looked around the airport bewildered. He had never been to the airport, let alone on a plane. Now he was getting nervous. He picked up his pace and walked faster and caught up to his mother.

"It's a nice place, this is. Can we go home now?" He said to her without taking his eyes off his surroundings.

"No, we are here and we are going to go through this together."

As they walked past the many gates, Matthew looked out the large windows and saw planes taking off and burn rubber as they landed. He then looked at the people waiting in the lounges and coffee shops. He had never been around these kinds of people before. The people at the airport reminded him of the people who travelled on the train. Some of the people at the airport slept on the benches like old Mr Lionel in the park who used a broken down cardboard box as a blanket.

"This would be a nice place for Mr Lionel, don't you think so mum?" He whispered to her. She didn't answer. She walked with her head up high and tightly held onto her hand bag.

They reached their gate forty-five minutes before takeoff. They checked in and followed the other passengers through a long tube to the plane where a very pretty airhostess greeted them warmly and showed them to their seats in economy class. She moved aside to let Matthew sit by the window.

"I don't want to sit by the window, mum."

"Yes, you do. I don't want you to miss a thing."

She could tell that he was nervous. When they both sat down, she helped him fasten his seat belt and then patted his hand and smiled at him. "You're going to be fine." She also looked nervous, but she was nervous about something else. When the engine started and the plane started rumbling down the runway, Matthew felt the vibrations go through him and it terrified him. Like a rock, he became stiff and he tried to dig his nails into the seat handles for dear life. The pressure of the plane taking off made him feel like his stomach had just dropped to the bottom of the soles of his feet. He tried to breathe steadily, but he was too terrified to remember how to breathe steadily. Without moving his head, he glared out the window and saw that everything was shrinking. The houses, cars and trees became like little toys. He squeezed his eyes shut and clenched his teeth and held his breath in. His mother put her hand on his arm. When the worst part was over, he opened his eyes and looked around him. He looked at his mother and she took her handkerchief and mopped the beads of sweat off his forehead. She smiled at him and he cracked a nervous smile. The pretty airhostess who showed them to their seats walked down the aisle and once she past them, Mrs Bellmont leaned in close to her son and whispered to him,

"We are going to Mtesa, our home which was called Graceland before our independence. Some white people still like to call it Graceland, but we...you should call it Mtesa, our free land."

"I know the history mum. You don't have to tell me. What the hell are we going there for?" he darted his eyes at her.

"It's where you're from. You should know where you come from. If you don't know where you're coming from, then you will never know where you're going in life. Besides, it's time you met your father."

"What the hell for!"

"Because he is your father whether you like it or not."

He looked away from her and stared out the window at the clouds that floated past the wings of the plane. A moment later, he softly asked her without looking at her.

"Do you still love him?" He did not want to see her face when she answered him.

"Yes." She answered softly. With an anguished whisper he asked,

"Why?"

"Sometimes we cannot explain how we feel about certain people." She said. This time, she looked away towards the aisle. He turned to look at her at that point and still wanted to understand.

"Aunt Catherine told me that he used to beat you, just like all his other women. I don't think I could ever forgive him for doing that to you." He reminded her. "What does he look like?"

With a shy smile she began to share with him what was stowed away in the memory of her heart.

"I remember him as clear as day. He was a tall white man with broad shoulders.....you have his build and his eyes, you know. No wonder those girls don't stop calling the house for you." This time she smiled at him with motherly affection. He tried not to smile, but the corner of his mouth stretched out and provedher right. "I used to be awfully jealous of any prettygirl who I thought would have any interest in your father." She reached into her handbag and pulled out a paperback book.

"What's that?" The cover of the book caught his eye.

"It's a book I want you to read before we get to Mtesa."

"Why?" He frowned.

"How much do you know about your country?"

"I am English, mum. I know enough about my country."

"No, you are African. You have been denying your heritage too long and it is about time you read about your own kind. This is a story about your family."

"Your family or my father's family?" He asked sarcastically.

"Actually, both. Your father may be white and I may be black, but we are both African. We are both from Graceland. The colour of our skin does not define where we come from. It is our beliefs and our heritage that define our character and where we come from."

He looked at his mother with different eyes. Even though he had heard her say that to him many times, this time she said it with passion and was intrigued by the way she ran her palm across the cover of the paperback book like it was a memoir. Matthew's curiosity got the better of him and could not hide that he had great interest in wanting to read the book.

"Who wrote it?" He finally asked.

"Munique."

"Uncle Munique? I didn't know that he wrote books."

"He doesn't. He only wrote this book and has never written again. I guess he felt that many stories had to be told without being biased." She glanced at him and was glad that she got his attention.

"What is it about?"

"I told you, it's about your family. Mainly about a boy much like you. I cannot tell you any more or else I will give the whole story away."

"Are you in the book?"

"Not really. Remember, I told you that I used to work as a housekeeper before you were born?"

"Yes."

"Well, it was your father's parents I worked for. That is how your father and I met. When I found out I was pregnant, I left their place and started working as a bar maid in town." Surprised, he asked her, "How come you never told me about this?"

"It wasn't important...For a while I was ashamed of what I was doing. I didn't want you growing up believing that your mother was nothing more than a simple black woman slaving after white people. But it wasn't until much later that I realized that there was nothing for me to be ashamed of. I was doing the best that I could and besides, in those days, black people were only allowed to take up working class jobs." She wasn't looking at him now. She kept looking down at the book in her hands and was lost in her memories of her past life. "The lucky ones were those who were very educated and had managed to save a lot of money to start their own businesses."

"Mum, I would never think of you as a simple black woman. You are my mother. You are the most hard working woman I know and you are more than anything to me." He reassured her and meant every word of it.

"I love you too...but you have to know that your father and I never married. Well, we talked about getting married, but we knew it would never happen." She concluded.

"How come you never told me all this?" He frowned with discontent and wanted to be angry with her for keeping so much from him, but he couldn't. She almost did not answer. She knew she had to give him the truth before he read the book.

"I was waiting for the right moment to tell you,...a time when you were old enough to understand...and I think this is now."

Once again, forgetting that he had asked her the same question, he asked her again.

"Are you in the book?"

"Yes....No, but Munique did right about your father." He narrowed his eyes and stared at the book in her lap, almost wanting to see what kind of man his father really was like. She knew that he loved reading and that it was the only thing that she knew he did privately away from his friends. They both were quiet and were absorbed in different thoughts. Matthew was curious to know why Uncle Munique would write about his father and not a good woman like his mother.

She prayed to herself and hoped that the book and their trip to Mtesa were going to help her son look at life differently. She was betting her whole life savings to make her son come right.

Like most of his friends, he never cared for school. Hanging out in the streets of London was cooler than sitting in the classroom full of preppie nerds speaking the queen mother's English. The truth of the matter was that he resented other children who did not accept him just the way he was. He never felt like he belonged. One thing that his mother knew was that he loved reading. He would hide in his room to finish reading the last few chapters of borrowed novels, history books and especially books about African writers.

Books have always been a great escape for him. His world required him to be street smart. He believed he was helping his mother make ends meet stealing and selling drugs on the streets. As long as his head was clear and never did drugs it was okay. He had seen how some of the other guys got messed up in the head with them. To her, it was equally bad. She blamed herself for her son's behaviour and denial of his heritage. She blamed herself for not teaching him enough. What was there to tell? She came from a small village and had moved to the city looking for work and only ended up working as a housekeeper, then a bar maid. The father of her child was a young rich boy who loved and abused women to his best ability. He was tall, domineering, and hated black people. Ironically, there was something about him that drew her to him. This obsession made her even more determined to prove to him that a black woman is as good as any white woman. She thought she was getting through to him until she fell pregnant. If his parents found out, they would have made her get rid of the baby. In fear of this, she left the Bellmonts and had not seen or spoken to him until that final day when he walked into the bar.

She was about five months pregnant at the time. She nervously made her way to his table and in her small voice she asked him what he would have.

"Whisky, no ice." He said without looking up at her. She walked away and as she waited for the barman to give her his order, she kept her eyes on him. He looked sad, she thought. He hung his head low as he slouched in his chair. Blankly, he stared at the same spot on the floor. She wanted to talk to him. She needed to ask him and know what was troubling him, but all that came out of her when she gave him his drink was, "Will there be anything else?" Her heart pounded when he slowly raised his hazy bloodshot eyes at her and hoarsely said, "No." He sipped his drink and went back to stare at the same spot on the floor. She stood and waited for a moment and realized that he had not seen her. He was far away.

She walked away to the back room of the bar to catch her breath from the fear and pain that struck her. She wanted to tell him who she was and tell him that she still loved him, but the words didn't come out. She could have said 'You once called me beautiful,' or maybe even 'I love you' one more time, but the words were trapped inside her. Once she caught her breath, she stepped back into the bar and promised herself that she was going to go back to his table to talk to him, but then noticed that he was gone. That was the last time she had seen him. Remembering where she was, she handed Matthew the book and he knew it was his chance to learn about his father. He took the book and opened to the first page and started reading.

PROLOGUE 1

Before 1850, the Europeans on the Cape of South Africa began to spread their influence through their missionaries and their traders. The Missionaries were recognized as the peace makers in the tribal regions that had the responsibility of trying to keep a balance of power in the Chiefdoms. They had brought their British influence, but at the same time, they learned and accepted the natives' way of life. They had hoped that their teachings of God's faith and the significance of Christianity would bring the tribes together. Other than being peace makers, they encouraged the Africans to trade with Europeans who grew interest in the Cape's wealth ofnatural resources. The Missionaries wanted thenatives to open their hearts and minds to another kind of people. Before they knew it, the British flocked to the Cape to settle and make a living for themselves while other Europeans flooded other parts of Africa. The Portuguese explored the east coast, the Germans settled on the west coast, and the people from Belgium settled in the Congo. By 1880, the British were permanent residents in South Africa (even though the Dutch had already been there) and were eager to explore further north into the "Darkest Africa."

In 1886, the British selected Mtesa as their port of entry into southeast Africa. Cecil Rhodes, the renowned British explorer, offered to conquer and claim the most profitable states of Africa, and Mtesa was one of them. Rhodes negotiated with the Chiefs in the different districts of Mtesa and gave them an offer they could not refuse. He promised to provide them with British troops who would protect them from Zulu warriors, the most undefeated African tribe that lived. In return, Mtesa was to give the British access to the shores to build ports where trade could be made.

As the years went by, Rhodes found a greater opportunity further north. He went on to explore the land on the other side of the Limpopo River and made plans to occupy Mashonaland. His goal was to "establish civilization in the place of barbarism." By 1890, Rhodes moved northeast and left Mtesa in the hands of the British Government. It was at this point that British miners and individual families came to Mtesa for its gold, diamonds, copper, and coal. The country which was only to be their port of entry for trade, became their new home. The De Beers Company and Kimberley Mines extended their profitable mining from South Africa into Mtesa. The money which the British South African Company made from Mtesa was used to explore north.

In some areas, individual miners would set up sites illegally without written documents. Those mines which were discovered by the government were confiscated, and those which were not claimed, continued to be self-supportive. Then there were those who vandalized and ran villagers out of their homes by burning their huts down and murdering, raping, and torturing the villagers just to dig up their land illegally. The villagers were helpless individuals whose estates were simply kraals made out of dung and twig fencing. Most of the times they were outnumbered and did not have the guns or armour the Europeans had. The only thing left for them to do was move into another clearing and start a new life. Missionaries went to the British Officials in the capital Mambosi, to speak on behalf of the villagers and tried to see what was being done for the villagers. Then again, when they found and caught the insidious highway men, they were either fined or imprisoned with minimum charges. Many changes were going on in not only Mtesa, but also in other southern African countries. The beginning of the 1900's was bringing change to the southern states. When Northern Rhodesia and Southern Rhodesia were established in 1911, Mtesa still lingered under the British Government. Africa had become Britain's new home and they started calling themselves White Africans. By October 5, 1920, Mtesa was renamed by the British Government as Graceland, a congenial blessing for the peoples of Africa. The religious dominance by the Missionaries and the business incorporated miners were there to stay. They themselves had ancestors who lived and died in the heart of what was now Graceland.

The Africans' barbaric behaviours were being altered by the immigrants. The missionaries set up churches and schools for the natives and had them adopt their language and Christian names once they were christened. They were taught that their faith in God was more important than anything else. Their nakedness and uncivilized customary manners were to be kept in their own circles, but to enter the world of "civilization," was a daring conception. Somehow, wearing shoes and many layers of clothing seemed to be a restricting way of life for the Africans.

The only Africans who had gained total and complete respect from the Europeans were the Chiefs and those who stood next to them in line. They were the only people who could officially give access to certain districts owned by the whites, and they were the only ones who mediated peace between the British and the Blacks. Those who lacked authority were recognized simply as Africans, blackies, barbarians, fools, coons, niggers, . . . In return, the Africans called the Europeans whites, Muzungus, Honkies, Mungeleshi, ...

In 1921, certain laws were being passed. It was to be officially known that Graceland had a full self-government -- although under the constitution the vested political power was exclusively in the hands of the white settlers. The United Kingdom vetoed any legislation contrary to African interests. With certain laws being established, certain changes had taken place. With only 7% of Africans employed, a law was passed to segregate the whites from the blacks, on African tribal lands. The only way Africans could live on any other parts of the land was if they became tenants on the European owned land.

By the time World War II came, the tension increased between the races and the cultural and economic ties grew stronger. They grew to accept each other as long as lines were never crossed. Those who took their chances on extending their limits instigated cultural and racial feuds.

Graceland, a country made up of many generations scarred with religious, domestic, cultural, economic and racial wars, was struggling to survive under one sturdy roof. Times were changing and the people were changing, but history had imbedded their traitorous segregated ways of life which in turn, became their beliefs. This is where the story begins. The lives of the people in Graceland.

Chapter One

Fhrom a distance they could see a light flicker in a small window on the second floor of the house they were walking to. The sun was almost behind the meeting point of the two mountains when the last bird glided across the auburn sky that was soon to become dark. Sarah took a deep breath, squeezed Kungulu's small hand in hers, and made him look up at her with his wondrous eyes.

"Is that the house mama?" He asked. She smiled at him to assure him that it was the house they were coming to start yet, another life. As they walked up the driveway, she remembered how her mother took her there just as she was taking her own son. The closer they got to the front door, the faster her heart raced and butterflies fluttered in her stomach. Before she knocked on the door, she put her small boxed suitcase down, wiped her sweating palms along her skirt, and smoothened back her hair under her little faded black hat. She then knelt down and wiped the dust off Kungulu's shoes with the inside of her skirt, and wiped the little beads of sweat off his forehead with her fingertips.

"Remember," she said softly, "only speak when spoken to." She rose to her feet and gently tapped on the door four times before Mary, a young black woman about Sarah's age, came to open the door. In her white cap and frilly apron, her welcoming smile died when she saw the appalling sight of a black refuge with her offspring practically clinging at her side. Her eyes trailed from their heads to their toes, making Sarah feel uncomfortable. To distract her, Sarah spoke out in her strong Bantu accent where she began to roll her R's at the beginning of a word and drop them at the end of a word.

"Is Mrs Bellmont in? .... She is expecting me. I am Sarah Zulu," she ignored the glare and continued "I am the new cook."

"The new cook,.... hmm. Wait he'e." She rolled her eyes and went to the study down the marbled hallway. When she returned, she followed behind Mrs Bellmont. Tall and lean, Mrs Bellmont stood before her just as she had remembered her, only that the years had gathered around her eyes and mouth.

"What's this?" She inquired and indicated to Kungulu with the palm of her hand.

"My son, mum..." softly and unexpectedly, Sarah found her voice.

"You didn't say anything about it."

"No, mum," she lowered her head, not of shame, but of fear of being turned away. "But I had no one to leave him with. He is my only family, and..."

"What about your mother?"

"She passed away last yea' when the road men came to plough through owa veelage. . . . . .when they fo'ced us out of owa homes, mum." Mrs Bellmont was aware of how bulldozers came and ran over huts and crops, leaving them in a pile of dust as their way of expanding the urban life.

"I see." She clasped her hands and looked down into the four year old's oval brown eyes, which stared back at her innocently. The full cheeks, small peach lips, and a complexion much lighter than the mother's, were simply irresistible. As Mrs Bellmont tried not to show her compassion, she turned to Sarah and replied, "Enough said I need you to start tomorrow. I have important guests coming Tuesday and you are the only one here. Keep the child out of sight and we won't have any problems, understood?"

"Yes, mum," She kept a straight face, but her heart was smiling with relief. She tried to hide the nervous quaver in her voice and followed Mrs Bellmont to the small servants' quarters behind the house.

That night when the African skies dwelled over their house, Sarah snuggled under a blanket wrapping her arms around her son. She heard him breathe deeper as her heartbeat put him to sleep. All she could think about was how she did not have to explain to Mrs Bellmont that her son's father was a white man she never knew. She remembered how Mrs Bellmont looked at Kungulu long and hard. She had studied his features, which were small, like the white man's, but Sarah was glad that he had her large dark African eyes that were eager to catch the sight of things from miles away.

She remembered how he was conceived. A white soldier had mounted her and had ignored her screams of agony and pain as he brutally raped her. When he had finished with her, he continued terrorizing their village with the other soldiers. She shut her eyes and erased the past out of her mind. If Mrs Belmont had asked her where the father of the child was, she would not have known what to say. The whites do not understand what it is like being a nothing in their eyes, she thought. She had come to believe that white women like Mrs Bellmont would not understand where a black woman was coming from and why she had taken certain paths in her life.

"White fo'ks will neva undastand." She mumbled underneath her breath. She knew that worrying about it would not help her struggle and fight to survive in her own country. She sighed, and soon she also drifted into a deep sleep, following Kungulu's breathing pattern.

As the cock crowed and the sun filled the horizon with its auburn glow, Sarah was already preparing breakfast for the Bellmonts. By 7:30a.m. breakfast was already set on the table and the Bellmonts were seated, except Charlie, their youngest son. They patiently and quietly waited until he barged in with his shirt half tucked in his trousers, which he quickly fixed before sitting down. He then jumped out of his seat remembering he had forgotten to kiss his mother. He kissed her softly on the cheek and sat back down again.

"Sorry mother,"

"I hope being away at school has not made you forget the rules around here. We are a family and I expect us all to eat together like a family." She scolded and then added "All meals."

"Of course." He said coolly, charming her as he always did.

"Now that you are out of school, what are your plans?" His father, a bona fide military man who always believed in self-reliance, inquired and wondered what his son, who he hoped would follow his footsteps, was planning to do with his life.

"I thought that I might come and work beside you so I could . . ." Before he could say any more, his father faced his palm at him in opposition and firmly said, "I am afraid that will not be possible. I won't allow it." Everyone looked at him in surprise. "You are a Bellmont and I expect you to build your own success like every Bellmont has done. You are expected to go out, find

24

work and a place of your own." His deep militant voice conveyed no remorse.

"Yes, father," was all Charlie could say. It was all he had ever said and was able to say to his father.

"Of course, you can stay at home until you find work." His mother glared at her husband and knew that he could not speak against her suggestion.

"Yes, of course, if your mother wishes for you to stay, you may." As he sliced the food on his plate, he changed the subject by turning his attention to his daughter sitting next to him. "So, Catherine, how's William? I spoke to his father yesterday and..."

"Don't even start with me about William Wisboe, father. I have no intentions of marrying that pompous Muzungu who only talks about how much he has and how much he is going to keep for himself." Her father frowned at the way she insulted her own race.

"I won't have you talking like that about your own kind," "He is not my own kind, father. He is nothing like me. At least I admit that I am African," "Darling, you are not African," her mother jumped in.

"I was born and raised here wasn't I?"

"Anyway, that is beside the point." her father broke in again "What is it about William that you don't like? I think he is a rather pleasant man."

"You don't think father, you just let words come out of your mouth and assume that what you are saying is right. Besides, what makes you think that I want to get married?"

"Because you are getting old," her mother noted the obvious and shrugged her shoulders blatantly.

"What if I don't want to get married, and what if I like my life just the way it is? Trying to preserve the wildlife is the best thing I have done in my life." She fiercely attacked her scrambled eggs on her plate with her fork and mashed them vigorously. As the anger boiled up in her, she tossed the fork in her food, threw her napkin from her lap onto the table, and stormed out. Mrs Bellmont looked at her husband and said,

"That is your side of the family coming out of her, George. She is as stubborn as you are."

"She is your daughter too you know."

"Oh George,..." As they continued arguing, Charlie quietly moved away from the table and joined his sister on the front steps of the house. He sat down next to her, took a deep breath and sighed.

"Boy is it great to be home. Nothing has changed at all."

"You are right about that. I thought that college would do you some good, like learning how to stand up to father and speak for yourself." The harshness in her voice made his smile die out as he remembered how angry his father always made him feel every time he tried to please him, but he was only pushed farther away from him.

"Of all people, you should know how I feel. I don't need you to criticize me when you damn well know how hard I try at whatever he thinks is best for me. But of course it is never good enough for him."

They both looked away from each other realizing thatthey were both starting up an endless argument which they had had a number of times. Catherine threw one arm around her brother's shoulders and patted his back.

"I guess we are in this together. Hmmm," she sighed "let's see," She smacked her lips and analysed their situation. "I am 25 and according to mother, I am a spinster, and you are 22 an unemployed bum. What successful children we are in not meeting our parents' goals." she said sarcastically. They both broke into smiles and shook their heads and laughed it off.

Changing the subject, Charlie spoke out in a more pleasant tone.

"We have a new cook, you know. I heard her come in last night."

"Really?" Catherine perked up with surprise

"What is she like?"

"Don't know. I just heard her talking to mother when she arrived last night. All I could make out of the conversation is that she came with a little coloured bastard. Mother wasn't too happy about it, because she was only expecting the cook and not her family. These blackies breed like rabbits, I tell you." "Don't be so judgmental. You haven't even met them yet. If it is any consolation, you are beginning to sound more like father." There was a tinge of anger and irritation in her voice that almost made Charlie hold back on what he was going to say next.

"I don't understand why you care for those blackies anyway."

"They are people too, you know. If you stick around a little longer, you will know what I am talking about." Before he could say anymore, she got up and went back into the house. As she walked to the back of the house, she heard a faint voice humming. It sounded like it was coming from the kitchen. She quietly made her way to the voice and saw a black woman standing over the stove singing to herself.

Catherine tried to get her attention by greeting her aloud. "Bwanji, mami," She clasped her hands together and bent her knees slightly. Sarah turned around and frowned at the white woman who was offering a black woman respect.

"Bwanji." she replied softly, and nodded her head. They both stepped towards each other and looked into each other's familiar faces. "Sarah!" The excitement in her voice made her throw her arms around her old childhood playmate.

"Hello, Catty!" She hugged her back tightly and fought back the tears of excitement. When they parted, they stood before each other smiling and not knowing what else to say.

"Twelve years," Catherine started. She looked at Sarah, a young woman with a slender body and glowing eyes. Sarah looked at her friend and saw a child in a woman's body. Her blond hair was loosely tied back leaving a few strands dangling along the sides of her face, her baggy beige trousers held up by suspenders, and thick brown Safari shoes defined her tomboyish look. They both laughed and hugged once more.

"How is your mother?" Catherine started once more.

"She passed away about a year ago,"

"Sorry, ... I didn't know."

"That's okay. Ever since she died, I only have one thing to live fo', my son."

"You have a son!" the excitement rose back in her voice.

"Yes, Kungulu. He is the one thing that makes me want to live. If you want to see him, he is in the back playing."

Catherine stood in the doorway that led to the back yard, and watched the boy as he played. She wondered where all the years had gone, yet life still stayed the same. She wondered what his future was going to be like. By his light complexion she wondered whether it would make his life easier if he passed for a white person, but then again, it would make his life more difficult because he was half-black. Choosing from the two sides was a conceptual factor in his life. Now that it was in the late fifties, life for the whites was good. A big house, pool, servants, and having control of the government were the luxuries of life which they were not ready to give up. As long as they kept the blackies under their nails and the Missionaries silent, there was peace. As long as lines were not crossed, people accepted their life styles in either urban or rural areas. Tension only rose when urban people wanted to expand and distribute their cities into the grasslands where the black rural families nestled in their huts by the riversides. Like Sarah's village, which was like most villages, where the Chief refused to clear out before a certain date, their huts and little gardens were bulldozed down into a heap of garbage.

Once they discovered diamonds, iron, copper, and gold, the hunger for wealth had rapidly expanded by burning savannah grasslands, blowing up mountainsides, and running down villages. Other than the richness of the soil, there was the wild life that was slowly but surely diminishing as poachers hunted them down for their skin and ivory.

The more Catherine thought about it, the more repulsed she was with her family who played a role in every conspiracy there was in the capital Mambosi. She had sworn to herself that she would never get involved in their wrongdoing.

Watching Kungulu finally catch a grasshopper in his small hands froze her train of thoughts and brought her back to what she was in the back yard for. She walked toward him as he carefully inspected the insect in his hands.

"I was never able to catch those grass hoppers when..." her voice startled him and made the grasshopper jump right out of his hands and quickly disappear in the thick carpet of grass. With his eyes wide and shy, he looked up at the tall white woman. "I'm sorry. I didn't mean to scare you." Catherine bent down next to him until their eyes were level with each other. "Come on, I'll help you catch another one." She raised her forefinger and whispered, "First of all, we need to be very quiet so we can hear," she opened her eyes and mouth exaggerating the expression of surprise when they heard the cricket rub its legs together. Catherine cupped her hand into the grass and the cricketing stopped. "I think I got it," she whispered. With her other hand, she cupped the bottom part of her left hand and raised her hands between her face and Kungulu's. She slowly opened up her hands and suddenly, the cricket sprang from her hands and down her shirt.

From a distance, Sarah watched her friend frantically dance the cricket out of her shirt. Kungulu started laughing and jumping up and down with excitement when he saw the cricket disappear into the grass again. They both started after it, laughing and leaping on all fours. Sarah hadn't seen him laugh like that since her mother past away. Without realizing it, she also began to smile to herself.

"Hello," A voice from behind her startled her. Turning around, she found herself face to face with a man of a familiar boyish look. "I missed out on breakfast, so if..." Charlie was suddenly caught by the familiar face he once knew so well as a boy. "...if you could fix me some eggs.....please."

"Yes, sa." She replied lowering her head as she moved passed him to fetch a pan from the cabinet.

"It's good to have you back, Sarah." He added. Rhetorically, she asked,

"Is it?" and without facing him she walked to the burner and turned it on.

"I will be in the sitting room. You can bring the food to me there." He grimly walked away with his hands in his pockets.

She carried the tray out into the sitting room without making a sound. Solemnly, she put the tray down on the coffee table in front of him. He gently grabbed her wrist and tried to get her to look up at him, but instead, she froze with her eyes fixated on the tray. When he released her, she turned and began to walk away.

As she did so, he called out to her, "Thank you," he said. He watched her walk away and wondered what kind of man had stolen her heart, but then again, there was a presence of fear in her eyes and a taste of anger in her voice. The little girl he used to tease and make her slave after him had grown up into a mysterious, but yet, fragile woman. If this was fifteen years ago, she would have answered him back and would have taken his racial slurs without shame. He had always thought that she would grow up to become the most respectable woman in her village. Where have the years gone?

Chapter Two

There was a bright white shimmer around the full moon that night. Little creatures lurked in the bushes and the crickets formed an orchestra in the grass outside Sarah's quarters. Kungulu restlessly lay in bed next to his mother unable to sleep.

"Be still. It's late and you should be asleep by now."

He was still for a moment, but in less than five minutes he was fidgeting again. "Mama," he started again, "I played with white woman today. It okay?" Sarah smiled to herself and cunningly answered, "Of course. Catty is owa friend." "But Mami always said to stay away from white fo'kes because always not'ing but trouble." He imitated his grandmother as he waved a finger in the air just as she always used to do every time she scolded him.

"Go to sleep Gulu." Sarah said. She wrapped her arms around him and pulled him close. She softly started to hum the familiar tune she knew would put him to sleep. He closed his eyes and let her humming fill his inner ear and to his heart. Like always, he soundly fell asleep within minutes.

She lay awake thinking about her father. After hearing Kungulu speak her late mother's words, she remembered how her father always promised her mother that he would give her a better life. Because her mother's family did not approve of their marriage, he wanted to prove them wrong by making it in the real world. He was an ambitious man who loved his wife and only wanted to give her the best. Her father, a man who was like most black men, had left the grasslands to become a part of the white man's world called Civilization. They were a group of men who were destined to live a lie. With their many hopes and dreams of living the rich white man's life, they took their whole life's savings with them to trade it in for a new life in the city. Unexpectedly, they found themselves living in shanty towns which were rundown neighbourhoods with houses built from scraps left around the area. Sarah's father was determined to rise and live the life of a king. He wanted to be served hand and foot, wear nice suits with those chokers they called ties, and drive a shiny black motorcar that rumbled like zebra's hoofs when it went down the dusty road. The harder he tried to become a successful man, the harder the white man pushed him back to his place. For the longest time, he could not understand why coins and paper money were worth more than anything. To him, money was of no value when he compared it to leopard skin or a herd of cows. When he found himself growing hungry at night, he finally realized the value of money. It was the money that was going to buy him that nice house, the black motorcar and the suit that money could buy. He then started looking into the positions that paid money, but there wasn't much luck in him getting a high paying job. First they turned him down because he couldn't speak English. Until then, he would lift bricks and carry cement bags on his back like all the other blackies. So, he went off and learned to speak enough to communicate with them. Upon his return, they turned him away and told him he needed to read and write English if he wanted to be an assistant manager. Burning the midnight oil, he stayed up late every night learning the alphabet and improving his grammar. The more hours he put into his studying, the fewer hours there were to find sleep. No matter how hard he worked at his day job, he still couldn't scrape enough money to save. There was either not enough money to keep him warm in the cold dry winter, or there was not enough money to send for his wife and four-year-old daughter. Every day he endlessly watched the sunrise and fall and the moon float over his head at night. There were a number of times he could have left and returned to the peaceful grassland, but he refused to return home as a failure. He was determined to prove everyone wrong. The day had finally come. He had saved enough money to send for his wife and daughter.

By the time Sarah and her mother arrived in the city, they were told by his friends that he had been shot in the neck while fighting with a white police officer.

"What was his crime?" Sarah's mother had asked.

"He was walking to work when this police man tripped him and made him fall in the mud," exclaimed a man who knew her husband well. "The bwana got mad, so he pushed the police man in the mud and they started to fight. Hm. Madam," he began to explain, "around he'e, you never strike a white man. The penalty is death. If you want his body, they rolled it in the ditch along with the otha men who died from the mine explosion."

Till the day she died, Sarah's mother never forgot how nonchalantly the man had told them of her husband's death. It was like listening to a story that did not make any sense. Sarah's father's death was just the beginning of the chapters of deaths in her family.

Coming to live in the city was the biggest adjustment Sarah and her mother had to make. They

35

had to put their village life and ways behind them and without much choice, were forced to adopt the Western life if they wanted to survive. This was also the first time Sarah was introduced to Christianity when she started to go to school. Like all other black children, she had to adopt a Christian name to use in school and drop her African name Maluba. When her mother found work at the Bellmonts, Catherine had become her first white friend. Together they played and shared stories about their separate worlds until Sarah and her mother had to go back to her village. Her grandfather was deathly ill. Before they left, the nine-year old girls held hands tightly like sisters.

Sarah remembered how Catherine had tried to explain to her that by having faith in God, her prayers would be answered and they would soon see each other again. "All I know is how to survive." Sarah had answered her. "What good is a spirit when it's dead?" "It's not dead, it's alive in you, your heart, you mind, and soul." Catherine rehearsed the words she had learned in Sunday school.

Chapters of her life flashed and flickered in her mind as she finally drifted off to sleep. Voices followed by a sudden rustle in the hedges, brought her back to consciousness. She sheepishly crawled out of bed and looked out her small window above her bed. She squinted her eyes and strained her ears to the dark shadows rustling in the hedges. She looked over at Kungulu who was soundly asleep, and quietly lit her kerosene lamp. She squeaked her wooden door open and picked up a hoe that lay outside her quarters. Bare footed, she made her way to the rustling noises. When the rustling got louder, she tightened her grip on the hoe and held the lamp stretched out in front of her. Pushing through hedges and with the hoe raised above her head, she was ready to bring it down on a prowler's head. She heard a woman scream and as she was caught by surprise, Charlie rolled off the woman with his trousers down to his ankles. It was Mary, the maid who had answered the door the day she arrived. Sarah never really liked her, only because she was so absorbed into the Bellmont's lives. Now she knew why. The guilty couple gathered their clothing and brushed the grass out of their hair. Not knowing what to do, Sarah stood there, lamp in hand and hoe still high above her head.

"SSSarah,..." Charlie stammered. He quickly pulledup his trousers and started buttoning his shirt. Sarah dropped the hoe and started back to her quarters. "Sarah!" He whispered loudly after her, and before she reached her door, he jumped in front of her nervously with his face still sweating. "Look, it's not what it looked like,....no, no," he stopped himself, took a deep breath, wiped the sweat from his upper lip with the palm of his hand and started again. "No, it is what you saw. I love her." He knew he wasn't only lying to her, but to himself. "Please, don't mention this to my family. Especially my father, it would kill him." Sarah blankly stared at him and said nothing.

"What you do is your business." Her voice was calm and cool "If you excuse me, I want to go back to bed." Charlie slowly stepped out of her way and she walked passed him into her quarters. As she began to close the door behind her, Charlie held his hand against it. She looked up at him and waited for him to say something, but he didn't. They stood there staring at each other for a few seconds that seemed like a moment. Charlie moved his hand away and Sarah eased the door shut to the night.

The following evening, Sarah was in the kitchen carefully placing a piece of parsley on her last dish for the guests. Mrs Bellmont nervously over looked her work and was satisfied. The other black maids, who were polished from head to toe, came in to take the food out to the dining room where the guests hungrily waited to be served.

The dinner was a success. Catherine and Charlie mingled and pretended to be having a good time andwondered how much longer they had to keep up the charade. Casually, Catherine managed to slip away into the kitchen to have a chat with Sarah.

"I can't stand those people. All they ever talk about is how much money they have and how much more they are going to make." She slouched at the kitchen table and felt the warm brandy filter her body as she downed her drink. "I tell ya, the only thing I enjoyed was the food. You cook better than anyone I know." She reached across the table and patted Sarah's hand. At that moment, Charlie came in flushed and was untying his tie.

"I will be damned before I ever become like those stuffy bastards." He complained. He pulled out a chair and stretched out next to Catherine. "You might think that after a few hours people would get tired of talking about themselves, especially that hairy woman who looks like a baboon." Catherine laughed and Sarah shyly lowered her head to hide the smile that grew on her face. He downed his drink and sloppily kissed Catherine on her cheek. He reached across the table for Sarah's hand, but she pulled away and tucked her hands underneath the table. Her immediate reaction surprised them all.

"Well," he sighed as he began to get up from his seat

"I think I will go outside for some fresh air." When he left, Catherine turned to her with reassurance.

"He doesn't mean any harm. Besides, I think he is interested in that one,... what's her name again?"

"Mary." Sarah spoke softly, and clearly. Catherine looked at her with surprise.

"How did you know?"

Sarah shrugged her shoulders and said, "I can tell by the way they look at each otha."

The day was growing dark and the cumulus clouds were beginning to roll over the mountaintops and shadow the land. The rains were coming. The thunder echoed in the sky and the lightning tore through the clouds and cracked like a whip striking in the dark. Softly, the rain pit patted on the ground, the pit pat then grew to heavy showers and with the wind, and they veered in all directions.

On the inside, the house was quiet, warm, and empty. Everyone had gone out except for Sarah, Kungulu and Catherine. Mr and Mrs Bellmont had gone away to visit some elite friends of theirs who own one of the largest exporting/importing companies in Katoma City on the coast. Mr and Mrs Bellmont had been gone for five days and were due back any day. Charlie had been gone all day and had not been home since that morning. At home, Catherine nestled in a blanket in the living room with a book in her lap. She was comfortably sitting in her father's leather chair by the window watching the rain fall and form puddles and little streams in the thick soil. Sarah and Kungulu comforted each other in the kitchen on a wooden chair that squeaked every time she rocked him in her arms. As she rocked him gently, the thunder gradually grew louder and when it cracked and boomed, Kungulu threw his arms around her neck.

"Shhh," she comforted him. "You know that next yea' you are going to have to start going to school and when you are in school, you won't have time to be afraid of the thunder and the lightning." Kungulu just shrugged his shoulders and buried his head in her chest when he heard the rain whip against the window.

Outside, the rain fell hard against the ground, almost making it hard to see two feet ahead. As the clouds clashed in the sky, a sudden clap of lightning lashed towards the house and a strong gush of wind flung the left window in the kitchen open. A gust of wind and rain dragged in the dry leaves from the outside and formed a small whirlwind in the middle of the kitchen floor. Sarah jumped out of the chair and put Kungulu to the side. She ran to close the window tightly and when she did, she barred it with a wooden spoon. Catherine came into the kitchen with the blanket wrapped around her tightly and her hair hanging wildly on her shoulders.

"You two all right?" Still in shock, Catherine's voicewas shaky and unsteady. Sarah turned to her and nodded nervously. "Come help me fix the window in the study. The tree outside must have been hit by lightning. It fell and broke the window."

"Are you all right?" Sarah asked as she noticed the bleeding scratch on Catherine's left cheek.

"Yes, yes, I'm fine." She pushed her hand away anddid not want to be fussed over, and she quickly led her to the study.

Sarah followed on after her and Kungulu tagged along behind them as he tried to keep up with their pace. When they got to the study, a branch had gone through the window and was hanging over the chair where Catherine had been sitting. There was glass and dry leaves everywhere and the wind and rain were still blowing about the room. Sarah and Catherine started to break the small branches off and throw them through the window. Remembering that her father had a thick roll of plastic, which he used to patch up the leaking roof in the study, Catherine ran down to the basement to fetch it. Feeling her way through all the boxes and things lying on the floor in the basement, she found the roll of plastic. Quickly, she and Sarah began to nail a large plastic bag over the broken window along the wooden window frame to keep the rain out. The thunder grew louder and the rain whipped even harder against the plastic trying to force its way in. Just as they finished nailing the last corner of the plastic into the frame, they heard the front door slam.

"Charlie, is that you?" Catherine called out over the noise of the whipping rain and wind. "Charlie?" She called out again as she walked intothe next room. "Char . . ." She stopped herself whenshe saw the man who was standing before her wasnot Charlie. It was a black man standing betweenthe door and the steps leading to the upstairsbedroom. He was soaked to the bone and as he stoodthere, he formed a puddle on the marble floor. Wide eyedand wild-eyed, he held a blunt knife in his lefthand and pointed it at Catherine.

"Please, I don't want to hurt anyone . . . I . . . I. . . need help." He sounded more threatening than helpless. He pressed against the right side of his stomach where his shirt was stained with blood. Not knowing what to do, Catherine and Sarah stood there motionless. "You madam, come he'e." He waved his knife at Catherine, "He'e!" He demanded. When he yelled, she flinched and then slowly took one step towards him.

"Please, put the knife down and let me help you. You are hurt." She said.

He started to bring the knife down and Sarah started to slowly walk towards him. He quickly changed his mind and instead grabbed her by the shoulders towards him. He wrenched her body close to his and held the knife to her throat. "No, trusting a Muzungu was what got me into trouble and now they are after me. Like a rabbit they are trying to hunt me down." He talked into her ear and as he did so, he studied her face with his blood shot eyes. The anxiety grew and nobody said anything in the short period of time that seemed like eternity. He sniffed her neck and smoothly fingered a lock of her hair and spoke into her ear. "So this is why the white man is ova protective of his woman. So sweet, so soft. I wonder what a Muzungu woman tastes like." Like a mad man, he smiled to himself and almost started to chuckle. Sarah tried to step forward, but he caught her at the corner of his eye and threatened to cut Catherine's neck if she came any closer.

Kungulu stood there with his eyes wide, scrutinizing what was happening to Catty. He watched the man grab her breast and fondle it pleasurably as he licked and sniffed the side of her face and neck.

"Please, don't hurt me," Catherine's voice trembled and without a whimper, she began to cry.

"Please!" Sarah blurted out distracting the man's actions.

"Shut up, you!" He pointed the knife at Sarah and gritted his teeth, "You are not'ing but a bloody African woman who is their slave. Look at you! Even your child is poisoned by their blood." He looked at Kungulu's light complexion with disgust and said to him, "You are not white. You are spoiled blood. You will always be a black man and a servant in the Muzungu's eyes and they will spit on your grave when you die little boy."

"Don't you insult my son." Sarah's voice was harsh and offensive. She pulled her son close to protect him.

"Didn't I tell you to shut up?" The man looked around himself anxiously and was wondering what to do next. Out of rage and frustration, he pushed Catherine at the foot of the stairs where she fell head first, landing on her chin. "Get up!" Fearing of what he would do next, Catherine slowly eased herself up using her elbows and knees. He pulled her head back by her hair and turned her over onto her back and straddled her at the waist. He winced and put pressure to his bleeding stomach. He soon forgot about his pain and he looked down at Catherine with his eyes on fire. With his bloody hand, he touched her face, her chin and her throat. He began to tear her clothing away and expose her flesh. Catherine screamed with terror and started waving her hands and slapping him wildly. He grabbed her hands and pinned them tightly above her head. She closed her eyes and began to plead and beg him to stop. Her screaming and pleading was what he wanted to hear. It excited him to see a white woman feel helpless. She was begging him, a black man, and a man of no status, to stop violating her. He couldn't stop now, he was in control. Her life was in his hands and he had the power to take it away from her. When she tried to squirm underneath him, he slapped her hard across the face a few times. Her hair flung around her head covering her face from left to right. Another one of her ear piercing screams fell upon the loud crack and boom of lightning. Unexpectedly, the man's body fell hard on top of her and involuntarily started to convulse and twitch. When he stopped, he was still. Once she saw and felt the blood trickle from his mouth onto her cheek, she knew the man was dead. She rolled him off of her body and looked up at Sarah who was standing before her holding a hunting gun in her shaking hands. Catherine forced herself off the steps and slowly took the gun from Sarah who had a tight grip on it. She then made her way to the closet near the front door and put the gun behind the coat rack where it had always been. Even when they were children, they remembered seeing it standing up right against the wall. The only person, who was ever allowed to touch it, was Catherine's father. It was his special gun that he used when he went hunting. Kungulu stood there without blinking an eye. The picture of his mother killing the intruder flashed in his mind again and again and again. The man fondling Catty's breast, the blood, the screams, the thunder and the rain and the dead body did not go away. He watched his mother and Catty on their hands and knees scrubbing and mopping the floor, making sure they did not leave any traces of blood. He watched them carry the black body outside and not knowing where they took it, they disappeared in the rain. As he was told, he stayed put and did not move. When they came back soaking wet from the rain, they found him standing in the same spot. They then made him promise not to tell anyone of the incident. He looked into the two women's faces and saw the same fear he felt when he heard the thunder. The sound of thunder and lightning became the least of his problems. He did not fear the thunder any more. When he went to bed that night, the thunder and rain became music to his ears. He listened to it and imagined God playing the drums in heaven and not the evil spirits he used to see rising from the dead. One day, he will also learn to play the drums as well as God did in heaven. How beautiful they sounded and how comforting they made him feel. When the thunder stopped to clap in the dark African skies, he fell asleep to the monotonous sound of the falling rain.

When the sun rose over the horizon, the cock crowed to the sight of a brighter day. The branches on the trees stretched out their limbs to catch the rays and shadow the ground underneath them. The puddles twinkled when the sun caught their surface and the birds glided quietly in the clear blue sky. The waking of a new morning had restored new life and a new beginning for everybody. The dark stormy night was long gone and so was the man who had broken into the Bellmont's house. He was not to be spoken of again. Kungulu played in the yard as he always had, Catherine sat at the kitchen table reading the paper and sipping her cup of tea while Sarah worked vigorously around the kitchen. Even though they all thought about it, nothing was said. Life had gone back to the way it was. Sarah started to hum the tune she had always hummed and Catherine listened to her soothing voice and felt more relaxed.

Charlie walked into the kitchen through the back door yawning with his hands stretched above his head.

"Ah, what a night. Did you hear that thunder last night?" He walked over to his sister and planted a kiss on her cheek.

"How could I have not heard it? It was so loud I couldn't even fall asleep." Catherine lied.

"Is there any coffee, Sarah?" He asked as he sat atthe kitchen table next to Catherine.

"Yes, sa. You want some milk with that?" She did not even turn to look at him when she asked him. She mechanically fetched him a mug and put the kettle on the stove.

"Yes, please. Sarah, there is no need for you to call me sir. We are practically family. I know that..." his

45

attention was drawn to his sister. "What ever happened to your face Cathy?" He fingered her cheek with the scratch and the bruise on her chin, which she had unsuccessfully tried to cover up with makeup. She flinched and automatically pulled her face away. She tried to be casual when she started to answer him.

"Oh that's nothing. I was sitting in the study last night when the lightning hit the tree by the window. It broke the window and the glass or the branch, I don't know which, nicked my face. It's nothing, really." She lowered her eyes into her mug as she gulped down some more tea and forced the real nightmare out of her mind. Without feeling the tea burn the back of her throat, she fought to play her role as the composed person she always was. "What time did you get in anyway?" She said raising her mug to her face.

"Right now." he said, "I stayed over at Jimmy's last night after we had a few drinks at the pub. I didn't see any point in coming home when the storm hit."

"I think that is the smartest thing you have done since you came home." Sarah placed the cup of coffee before him and went on doing what she was doing. "Very funny." He played along with her sarcasm. "I wish father could give me the same praise as you always do."

"Don't get me started," Catherine said.

"You're right. Might as well enjoy the moment before they come home." Just as he was taking a sip from his mug, the front door slammed.

"What the devil happened to the window in the study?" Mr Bellmont's voice carried into the kitchen.

"Damn. I spoke too soon." said Catherine.

When they walked in, Charlie got up from his seat and over exaggerated to greet them with his arms stretched out. "Mum, dad. How was your trip?" He kissed his mother warmly and she cringed at the sight of his scruffiness.

"Just fine, but you better go and have a wash. I won't have my son looking like that. What if we were to have guests?"

"Yes, mother." He gave her a loving smile and kissed her again. He looked at his father who did not even comment on his appearance.

"Yes, yes, listen to your mother." His father waved his hand at him and as he had promised his wife, he prevented from saying anything too critical to Charlie. It definitely took Charlie by surprise when he didn't say anything. "Well, don't just stand there. Do as your mother says." he added.

"Yes, dad." He gratefully walked past them and marched on up the stairs.

"And what happened to you?" Mr Bellmont studied his daughter's face when he held it up towards him.

"It was from the bloody window in the study. I was reading in the chair when the lightning hit the tree which broke the window."

"You all right?" asked her mother.

"Yeah. Just a little shook up from the excitement."

"Well, as long as you are all right." Relieved, her mother sat next to her and continued to examine her face.

"Enough about my little escapade. How are the Clarks doing? Are they going to come see us sometime?" Catherine was always good at changing subjects when it was necessary, but today a little bit more effort was needed. Instantly, her mother's mouth rolled on and on about their visit and how hot it was.

"Being by the shore is really discomforting. The humidity from the sea just circles around you endlessly and the fans are useless. . ." Catherine wanted so much to tell her mother what had happened. She listened to her voice, but the words just seemed to be lingering in the air. Catherine glanced towards Sarah and looked for some sort of reassurance or maybe even a sign to let her know that she was doing fine, but there was no response. Sarah was too frightened to look at anyone in the face. She continued to focus on what she was doing by the sink and her hands worked rapidly and accurately as she pealed the potatoes. They both knew they had handled the situation quite well, but deep inside, they both prayed that nobody would ever have to find out. They both knew the penalties for a black woman killing a man. She would be imprisoned and the chances of walking out of prison alive and sane, were slim. Of course the interrogation would be traitorous and painful. The physical torture and beatings she would have to experience was more than she would be able to take. She had a son to raise and with her being gone, there would be no one to take care of him. Catherine had offered to take the responsibility of shooting the intruder, but Sarah had refused. It was best to bury everything and forget about it. It would be weeks or even months before they found the dead body that was buried behind the barn shed. Once they found a dead black man's body rotting away in the hot sun, he wouldn't be worth worrying about. Then the officials would start to think that whatever he did, he must have deserved it. No further investigation would be made and the case would be closed. Maybe they should have called the police and let them handle it. No. It has been done and nothing more can be done to change the past. Where did that man come from anyway? The Bellmont's house was three miles away from Mambosi, and twenty miles from Pangani City, an all black colony.

Upstairs in the passage, Charlie was on the phone gripping the receiver tightly and had been holding it close to his lips. "What do you mean you lost him?" the voice on the other line sounded hoarse and muffled in Charlie's ear.

"It was dark and it was raining hard. Besides, he was hit, and there is no way he could have found help because we were miles away from any house or hut."

"Does Johnny know?"

"Yes, he was with me."

"Now listen carefully. Johnny told me to tell you that that was only a drill. The next one is going to be the real thing. Be ready tomorrow.

"Did he say where we would be meeting?"

"Just sit tight and we will let you know."

There was drilling of jackhammers and clanging of sledgehammers on the rocks on the mountainside where gold was said to be found. The men worked vigorously as their hands and feet blistered in the hot sun. Charlie made his way through them to a suntanned, grim and grungy looking white man who was monitoring his workers on the site. He stood broad shouldered with his arms folded and a horsewhip in one hand. Just when he saw one of his men slacking, he decided to go and threaten him with his whip. In his long strides, he walked over to the elderly man who was kneeling down by a bucket and was just about to take a drink of water out of the ladle.

"You, get up! I don't pay you to take rests whenever you like. Get up!" He raised the whip above his head enough to make the man flinch and quickly get back on his feet. "You, ova theya!" He yelled across the work site, "Don't drink too much wata. Leave some foe the others." With the sleeve of his shirt, he wiped the sweat off of his forehead and swatted the flies away with his whip. "These bloody nigge's, . . ." he mumbled before raising his head to his unexpected visitor. "Well, I'll be damned." He said surprised. He wheezed out his chuckle and threw his arms around Charlie. They gripped hands and patted each other on the back.

"Good to see you Johnny." Charlie smiled.

"They really polished you up ova theya, didn't they? Dressing and talking like a real Englishman, eh? Good thing you left when you did or you would've turned out to be like me. More and more each day I sound and look like them blackies." As he pointed to his own suntanned face, he wheezed out another chuckle.

"I didn't have a choice. You know what my old man is like. It's either I be like him or be damned." Charlie teased himself.

"Yes, well, I don't think I could or would want to leave Graceland. Even if it means living in the same country as my drunken' father, this place will always be my home. Come. Let's get out of the blooming' heat."

Johnny showed Charlie to his wooden shack of an office back down the hill. They sat on squeaky leather chairs and drank ice water as the summer air thickened around them. A small fan on the side table whirled from left to right and only blew the hot air around the room.

"So, you he'e for good?" Said Johnny as he sat back in his chair.

"Seems like it. I can see that business has been good to you."

"Don't let those workas fool ya. If those missionaries don't protest in my area, I will be fine." Yes, I heard about them. They have already put three industries out of business."

"Yes, but that is only in the south in Kamputo. It used to be the biggest copper-producing city in Mtesa. Now look at them…Nothing. The missionaries are slowly making their way up he'e. It's worse than what it used to be you know. To save my ass, I had to agree to give my workas a salary. Yes, we all have to pay the blackies to work now." He sipped his ice water and twirled the glass and made the ice clink against it. "I tell ya, these nigge's don't deserve to get paid. Well, enough about me." He swivelled his water and mopped his forehead with his sleeve again. "I know you didn't come here to talk about the latest news in the paper. You have something on your mind, no?"

"You still can read me like a book." He took a deep breath and clasped his hands together. "I need a job."

"What 'bout your father?"

"He wants me to start on my own. How can I start on my own if I don't have anything to start off with?

"Right. What kind of job did you have in mind?"

"Anything to get me off my feet."

"I see." Johnny said thoughtfully. There was a brief moment of silence until he said, "There is a project that I have been trying to start for a long time, but I just haven't had the time. If everything goes as planned, money will be flowing in like the River Nile. If you are willing to help me get this thing started, I will split the profits with you fifty-fifty. You interested?"

"What is this project?"

"Well, I can't tell you what it is unless you are willing to risk your life. It's all underground stuff." He saw that Charlie was looking pensive. "Come on, it will be like old times."

"You're losing me Johnny."

"Okay, okay. Because you are my good friend and I know that you and I could make a good team, I will tell you. I call it Mutoto wa Mutoto." Charlie looked at him confused and tried to see what dirty scandal his friend was up to. "Let me explain,..." Charlie listened attentively and knew that what he was getting himself into was going to make his father's head spin. But the hunger for adventure and the itching palms for money made him want to do it even more.

"Do you want to think about it?" Johnny said after he finished explaining it to him. "No." Charlie was certain with and did not want to have any second thoughts about it. The Mutoto wa Mutoto conspiracy was about to go down and when it did, it was going to change his life. It was time for him to do something for himself, something that he wanted to do and not what his father expected for him to do.

On his way home, Charlie passed through town and blankly looked at the people making traffic in the market place. He disappeared into the crowd and found himself in a section of the market place where goats, oxen, and horses outnumbered the occasional car that rumbled past, leaving a cloud of dust behind. Men and women stood behind their wooden tables thrusting their fresh vegetables and fruits in the faces of their customers. One woman raised a limp fish in Charlie's face and tried to catch his attention, "Look, fresh fish. Sa, look! My husband caught it today two awas ago." Charlie brushed the fish out of his face and walked on passed the strong aroma.

"Bananas, mangos! He'e, fresh!" another vender yelled in his direction. Charlie felt he had enough. He crossed the street and started staring into the window of a shoe store. When he turned to walk away, a little black boy ran into him and fell and scraped his knee.

"Sorry, sa." His frightened eyes could not look him in the face.

"Hey! Stop that boy! A short stubby white man ran in their direction. Charlie could see that he had difficulty carrying his weight. From the way he was running, it was painful to see him sweat and pant as he pushed his way through the crowd. "That little thief! Stop Him!" the fat white man called out again.

"Sa, I didn't take not'ing," The little boy pleaded with begging eyes to Charlie, hoping he would help him. "...please sa, I didn't do not'ing." All Charlie could see before him was a filthy little blacky griping for something he wasn't going to get. The fat man pushed Charlie aside and grabbed the boy by the arm and shook him aggressively. The fat man's shirt clung to sweat patches on his back and armpits as he bent down to bring his face close to the boy's face.

"You owe me boy. Your job is not finished yet. I pay you by the hour and I will let you know when you are done working."

"But sa, the smoke in the mines is making me sick," His voice was small and pleading. The fat man's backhand flew across the boy's face and made his fragile body fall to the ground.

"Don't talk back at me, you little nigger!" He grabbed the boy by the arm once again and dragged him away. Charlie stood and speculated along with the other people on the sidewalk. He watched and learned. He watched, indulged, and did nothing. He turned around with his hands still in his pockets and walked on down the street.

From across the street in the market place, another white man watched and looked on after Charlie. He put one hand through his sweaty sun bleached hair and covered his head with a brown hat. A woman at one of the stands broke his gaze by handing him his bags of groceries. Before he could reach into his pocket and pay her, a bucking horse caught his attention.

"Wooah!" The African was trying to keep his grip on the reigns. He tugged at them as he stood by the horse, but the horse only got more frantic. He raised his fore legs, neighed and made the African lose grip of the reigns. The African lost his balance and fell back in front of the horse. The horse raised its hooves again, but this time, it stomped on his right leg. The man screamed when he felt the bones in his leg crunch underneath the hoof.

The man with the brown hat dropped his groceries, grabbed the reigns and tried to calm the horse down. When the horse stopped bucking and neighing, he tied the reigns to a post. He looked at the African's leg that now was covered with blood and looked disfigured.

"You all right?" said the man with the brown hat.

"Sa, my leg,...sa," He clenched his teeth and tried to reach for his leg which throbbed from the pain and the numbness was beginning to rise to his thigh. He man with the brown hat threw his arms underneath him and carried him down the street. While he tried to balance him in his arms, his hat fell off and his sun-bleached hair curtained his face. Without knowing where he was going, he turned the corner into a veterinarian's clinic. He threw the swinging doors open and as he staggered in with the man still in his arms, one of the doors swung back against the man's leg. The African

54

screamed with agony and didn't even try to hold back the tears.

"Is there a doctor around here?" called out the man with the sun-bleached hair. The humidity in the room clouded his mind and made his face throb with redness. The well-educated black receptionist jumped from behind her desk and stood in front of them.

"You can't bring that man in here."

"Look," he pushed on past her into the back office where there was a long flat stainless steel table with towels on it. "This man's life is worth more than a gazelle's." He laid the man on the table and turned to the receptionist. "Where is the doctor?" His face glowed from the heat as he pushed his hair back from his face.

"Please, you are not allowed back here." She followed on after him as he took off to search for a doctor.

"I am not leaving until I find someone who can treat this man!"

Catherine was doing some paper work when she heard the noise outside her office. She got up to open the door, and before she could even reach for the handle, the door flung open.

"Are you a doctor?" he blurted out.

"What is going on here?"

"Are you a doctor?" he refrained.

"Yes, what's all this about? What is going on?"

"Come with me." He grabbed her by the arm and retraced his steps back to where he left the wounded African. Catherine snatched her hand back and said, "I can walk by myself, thank you." she glared at him and held his gaze and the receptionist noticed how the tension began to grow between them.

"Come on then." the man demanded.

"Madame," the receptionist started, "he brought in a man with a broken leg and I told him,..."

"A what!?! What were you thinking, bringing a man in a veterinarian's office?"

"Look, there is no time. He is losing a lot of blood and this was the closest place I could bring him to." He walked over into the room where the patient was. He stroked the African's sweating forehead and reassured him that everything was going to be all right. "Don't worry bwana; the doctor is going to fix you up." Catherine glanced at the state of the man's condition and the way the blood continued to flow from his leg to the table and onto the floor.

"May I speak with you in the next room, please?" She addressed the man. The whole situation made her nervous. He followed on after her to the reception area where she began to speak more calmly.

"The man has a broken leg."

"How very observant of you, doctor. Can you fix it?" His sarcasm made her angrier. Instead, she bit her lip and chose to calmly talk to him.

"All the animals I treat usually make it, but those that come in with legs this severely broken are put to sleep. Because I am a vet, I am not obligated to treat this man."

"A man is bleeding to death in there and all you can tell me is that you would rather treat a dog than a man? Have some compassion woman."

She finally was not able to hold her cool any longer. She gritted her teeth and snapped like a twig.

"Don't tell me how I should or should not feel. I am aware that the man needs help, but I can't help him." The anger began to boil in her when he turned his back to her while she was talking. She saw him clench his fists and mumble something underneath his breath.

"What did you say?" she asked. He took a deep breath, turned around and answered,

"Look. To me, a doctor is a doctor, . . ." Their conversation was interrupted by the African screaming in agony in the next room. "Do something woman!"

She pointed a finger at him and told him to keep his post. She went into her office and made a phone call. Fifteen minutes later a middle-aged white doctor with wire rim glasses and a black leather bag walked into the clinic. The receptionist showed him to where Catherine had already started to clean the wound. With eyes wide, the doctor said, "This man is black." "Yes, I know." Said Catherine. "You aren't serious," "Very." She finally raised her eyes up to the paralyzed doctor and with all seriousness she said, "You aren't going to let the colour of this man's skin stop you from saving his life, are you?" The doctor said nothing.

"He has lost a lot of blood." added Catherine.

"Catherine," the doctor finally spoke, "you know that I work at a white clinic and if they find out about this, I could lose my job."

"Well then get out." She walked over to him and levelled her eyes with his. "If you aren't going to help me, then get out!"

"How dare you speak to me like that? I have known you since. . ."

"You have known me long enough Dr Johnson. What are you going to do? Tell my father? You just take your egotistical self back to your white clinic."

He stood in shock and didn't know what to say.

"Get out you racist pig."

"You haven't heard the last of me Catherine. I will not have you speak to me like that." He stormed out of the clinic and Catherine went back to finish cleaning the wound.

The moment the doctor left, in came the man with the sun bleached hair.

"What did you say to him that made him leave so quickly?"

"Something that I should have said a long time ago."

"There is no time to settle old conflicts when there is a man fighting for his life..."

"That doctor refused to treat him because he is black. My main concern is the welfare for this man and the last thing I need is you to tell me that I have no compassion. If you really want to know, I am blooming' scared because I have to take his life in my hands. So if you don't mind, step outside for a while so I can see what I can do for him."

He was caught back by her response and instead of answering back; he chose to quietly go back to his seat in the waiting room where he studied the anatomies of different animals on the walls. Each minute seemed like an hour and the air never seemed to cool down. He sat and thought about the woman doctor and how tempered she was. Never had he met a woman who was attractive and yet so vulgar at the mouth. The combination excited him and the thought made him smile to himself.

"Excuse me, sa." His thoughts were interrupted by the little voice that came from a small boy of about seven. He stood next to him and woke him from his daydream. The boy carried a bag of groceries and was tipping his head back enough so he could see from under the oversized brown hat the man had dropped in the street. The man tilted his head to the side to get a better look at the boy's face.

"Well, hello there." he inspected.

"Mama Tol' me to bring dis to you. You drop in the street." He handed him the groceries and with his hands free, he was able to push the hat away from his face. The man began to reach into his pocket to pay.

"No,"

"But I didn't pay for them."

"I know. Mama wants you to have them. She sees you help a bwana. Zikomo, she says."

"Zikomo." The man replied. The boy put the hat over the man's sun bleached hair and smiled. The man took it off and placed it back on the boy's head.

"I think it looks better on you." They both smiled and they shook hands.

Catherine watched them from the side in the doorway and she also found herself smiling too.

Catherine walked into her office rubbing her templesfeeling a headache coming on. It was going to be along day. She glanced at her appointment book andrealized she was to have been in Mpolo a half-hour ago. Unfortunately, there was no way of getting out of it. She had made the appointment weeks ago and the other veterinarians from South Africa were probably already there waiting for her. Mpolo was a good thirty minutes' drive from Mambosi and the thought of driving in the hot sun and dusty road exhausted her. With or without a throbbing headache, she had to go. She grabbed her bags and told her secretary to hold off any other appointments until tomorrow, and was out the door.

While driving through the dusty savannah grasslands, she thought about the usual routine of being out in the heat for hours collecting data on the elephants which were being hunted down illegally for their ivory. The smell of their immense dead leathery bodies drying up in the sun swarming with parasites was a thought that made her stomach turn. It was something she was supposed to be used to by now, but every time she encounters it, her stomach turns. Once she arrived in Mpolo, things were quiet. She parked her jeep next to the other two jeeps under a large shady tree, which also shadowed the little office with a thatched roof, open windows with thin small blue and white curtains. As she walked in, three men lay lazily on their backs. Two were in hammocks and one of them lay on top of a desk. They all had their hats covering their faces. She cleared her throat to get their attention, but none of them budged.

"Hello, Dr Bellmont." said a voice from underneath one of the hats. The potbellied man who lay on the desk lazily pulled himself up to get a better look at Catherine.

"Sorry I am a little late." she said, and shook his hand warmly.

"Oh, that's all right. It gave us some time to catch up on some sleep. We have been on the road since yesterday.""And whose idea was it to drive when we could have flown?" Another man rose from his hammock and dusted himself off with his hat. "Hello, I am Dr Jones. Just call me Jones." he stretched out his hand and shook Catherine's hand warmly.

"I'm Dr Russell, Russell is just fine." said the potbellied man. "And that over there is Father Munique. He got us here when we got ourselves lost near a herd of buffalo. He works in the Kukui Tribe a few miles from here. Have you heard of them?"

"Yes, yes, I am familiar with them."

"If it weren't for him, we wouldn't be here."

Russell chuckled and his belly shook over his trousers as he securely pulled up his trousers by the thick leather belt he was wearing.

Catherine looked over at Father Munique and knew that there was something familiar about him, but she couldn't tell what it was. He silently lay there with his hat still over his face and his hands folded over his stomach.

"Father Munique," Russell started "Dr Bellmont is here." All four doctors stood there and watched the young priest swing his legs from his hammock and scratch his head lazily. He pushed his sun-bleached hair back and covered it with his hat. He greeted Catherine with a small smile as he tipped his hat to her.

"It's nice to seeing you again, Dr Bellmont." "You two know each other?" asked Russell. Catherine cleared her throat and tried not to look at Father Munique straight in the face when she said, "We met the other day in my office." She nervously started to fidget and her cheeks flushed with embarrassment. The man was a priest and she felt guilty for the way she had talked to him in her office.

"Isn't it a small world, eh?" said Russell.

"Well, then gentlemen. Shall we?" Catherine eagerly walked out of the hut and jumped into her jeep.

"If it is all right with you, Father Munique would have to ride with you. We are only dropping him off at the village a few kilometres from here."

"That's fine." Catherine said, but deep inside, sheregretted agreeing to give him a lift.

They worked in the area for the next few hours and right before the sun set, they started off down the dusty road to drop Father Munique off at the nearby village. Father Munique and Catherine drove in awkward silence untilCatherine broke it with an apology.

61

"I would like to apologize for my behaviour the other day in my office. My language and tone were uncalled for and I apologize."

"Just because I am a priest, it doesn't mean that you have to act any different around me. Believe me; I do know what it is like working under a lot of pressure." He reassured her. They road in silence again until he broke the silence by asking her about the fading bruises on her face.

"I got in a fight." She lied.

"Why doesn't that surprise me?" he mumbled under his breath, knowing that she didn't hear him.

"What?" She said.

"Nothing." He said while looking the other way.

When they got to the village, Munique showed the doctors around and showed them what types of reconstruction and farming he had been helping the villagers with. Two women wearing printed fabrics wrapped around their waists and heads greeted them with two bowls of goat's milk. It was a clean and pleasant little place with goats and children running around the mud huts. The Chief, a man wearing leopard skin as a sash and head wrap, asked them to join the villagers for a festive meal in their honour. To refuse would be an insult, and Catherine always loved such ceremonies where huge plates of food would be served and afterwards, they would join in the traditional dances to the music of the beating drums and the bells tied to their ankles. That was the kind of spirit of Africa she loved so much.

That afternoon, the veterinarians and Father Munique sat around in a large circle feasting on cassava, oxen, and vegetables. Munique became the mediator for the Chief and the doctors while Catherine used her broken language to talk to the women. They put beads around her neck and flourished her hair with purple flowers and combs. Munique watched her at the corner of his eye and noticed how she had a way with people and how they loved her too. He drew his attention to the Chief and doctors and continued to translate.

"The Chief says that last night, four white men came and stole his son."

"Why would they want to take his son? Did they want something else in exchange?" James asked.

"Actually, no. This land is not worth anything. It is only good for growing a few crops and nothing else. They said that if he didn't do what they requested, they were going to come back and burn down the whole village. He says that his son goes to the big city to study, to become a good doctor. He was only visiting his family when they came for him," Munique translated. The Chief was quiet and Munique told the doctors his part. "I was here when it happened. I just wish I could have gotten a better look at them, but they hit me on the back of my head and I passed out." Munique rubbed the back of his head, still feeling the bump that had made his head throb earlier.

The day drew darker as the sun hid behind the grasslands, leaving its lingering warmth fade into the night. The villagers made a fire in the middle of the clearing and the food was cleared. Four men began to play the drums and their fermenting beer was being passed around in large wooden jars with hollow sticks for straws. Some women dancers began to dance and tell the story of two young lovers from different villages who could not be together because their families were at war with each other. Other men and women joined in the dance and one of the women grabbed Catherine by the arm to have her join in the fun. The other doctors sat and watched and laughed along with the others as Catherine tried to follow their steps. Her drunkenness overwhelmed her and her co-ordination was a little off. She finally plopped herself down on the ground next to Munique huffing and puffing, but she was still smiling and clapping her hands to the music. The jar of beer was passed to her and she took a large gulp of it through the straw. Watching this, Munique decided to warn her.

"You better take it easy on that beer. It is stronger than you think."

"I think you are right. Here." She handed him the jar, and he shook his head.

"I don't drink. A lot of people are always surprised to hear that because I am German." She took another swig of the beer and judging by her unsteadiness, Munique decided she was drunk.

"I would have never guessed that you were German." She tried not to slur.

"I was raised in South Africa. I feel that I am more African than German."

"I know what you mean. Africa is also my home. It's all I know." They talked over the loud music and just when she was about to say something else, she felt queasy and ill. She jumped to her feet and ran behind a hut and started vomiting. Munique followed on after her and tried not to laugh and refrained from telling her that he told her so about the beer. He offered to put her up for the night in his hut, but she refused. She had to get home before it was too late.

"You must be mad wanting to drive home this late. It is almost dark."

"I am not mad, just a little drunk."

"Even a better reason why you shouldn't drive."

"Well, okay. Just because I am not capable to drive, I will stay." As she swayed before him and gave him a chiding expression she said, "Will you put me to bed?" He laughed at her childlike manner and guided her to his hut where he took her shoes off and tucked her in before she mumbled herself to sleep. He watched her lay there and he studied her face. He reached out his hand and gently pushed her hair out of her face with his fingertips. He smiled to himself at how sweetly and soundly she slept. She was like an angel. He lay down next to her and continued to watch her sleep. A little while later, he went back out to join the celebration. Sometime later when he returned to his hut, Catherine was still sound asleep. Although peoplewere dancing and beating on the drums outside, hestill tried to be quiet as he slipped his boots off. He tiptoed to his side of the bed and as he comfortably lay down, Catherine rolled over and through her armaround him. Although she was still asleep, a certainfear rose up inside him. He carefully took her arm off his chest and placed it on her side. The hut was so small there wasn't anywhere else for him to move. Instead, he lay there staring at her beautiful face and slowly started to reach his hand out to it. 'No, I shouldn't,' he thought to himself. He pulled his hand away and took a deep breath and started reciting theHail Mary three times to himself. He sat up next toher with his knees drawn to his face. He took another look at her and then quickly buried his head between his legs and tightly shut his eyes as he fought thesinful image out of his head. He tried to concentrateon his prayers, but the music and dancing outside his hut and the woman lying next to him distracted him and made him feel weak.*"Please God, give me strength."* He picked up his bible and began to read aloud to himself until he fell asleep. The next morning, Catherine woke up to thesound of a woman pounding grains with a traditional mortar between her legs. She found herself curled upnext to Munique and was close enough to feel and hear his heartbeat. She quietly got up and slipped her shoes on hoping he wouldn't hear her. She crawled out of the hut squinting her eyes towards the sun which shown on the little village slowly coming back to life. Two women walked by her carrying sugar canes on their heads, followed by another woman carrying a large black pot of river water on her head. Behind them trailed two little naked boys with round bellies running to catch up to them. The relaxed atmosphere made her want to stay there forever, but she knew she had to get back to her suburban home and city life.

She didn't want to wake Munique who was still snoring, and instead she decided to leave quietly. She said good-bye to the Chief and thanked the women for their hospitality and promised them that she would soon return for another visit.

When Munique woke up with a crick in his neck, Catherine was gone. A sudden disappointment came over him and he knew he had to see her again. No. He's a priest. He has already given his heart and soul to the church. But last night he was tempted to put his arms around her and hold her and become a part of her. The sense of wanting to experience a sense of passion and comfort with Catherine made him feel good inside. He had never felt this way about anyone before.

He rubbed his eyes with the palm of his hands to erase the image out of his mind. He must resist the temptation. "Please God, forgive me for I have sinned," He prayed to himself "give me the strength."He promised to himself that he was not going to think of her or see her again. But little did he know that there was more to come in the near future.

Two weeks later, Catherine had returned to the village with Gulu. In the fewer years Gulu and his mother had been living with them, Gulu was only exposed to the city life and the white suburban homes. Her immediate intention, so she said, was to expose the ten year old boy to the other life of Africa so he could be in touch with his heritage, but the truth was that she longed to return to the real Africa for herself. She liked the sense of freedom and the ability to follow time by the rising and setting sun. They found Munique chopping wood with two other men under a shadowing tree. Seeing her again made his heart race. He continued chopping wood and at the corner of his eye, he could see her approaching with a young coloured boy he had never seen before.

"Hello, Father Munique. I brought a friend of mine to come and see how village life is really like and I was hoping that you could show him around.

"It is rather busy around here." He said between chops.

"I could help you out if you like. It is what I am here for." Gulu spoke maturely and Munique saw the eagerness in his will to help him. He stopped chopping wood and wiped his forehead and the nape of his neck with a rag. He knelt down before Gulu and asked him what his name was.

"Kungulu, sir." He said.

"Well, Kungulu. You look like a pretty strong young man. I think I could use another hand." They shook hands and returned smiles.

"I guess I will leave you two gentlemen to get to your work. I had promised the ladies that I would visit them." Catherine was glad that the boys hit it off pretty well on their first encounter. She kissed Gulu lovingly and left feeling good about herself. Munique was surprised to see the loving action between the two of them and made him want to jump to conclusions, but then again, it was none of his business.

Kungulu helped Munique stack up the chopped wood and carry some of it back to the village. Their next task was to go spear fishing with the other men and boys who were already at the water hole. Kungulu felt as though he was the centre of attention because they had never seen a coloured boy before. His light brown curls and small features threw them off. They all agreed that he was going to grow up to be very popular amongst the women and would have many wives. Kungulu then decided that he liked the village life. After talking to the men, he felt like this was where he belonged - a world of no segregation, and nakedness was acceptable. It was nothing like the city that limited his space and friends.

As they walked back to the village, Munique explained to him what village life was like. It totally disconnected itself with the city life.

"Everything that goes on in the city is left in the city, and everything that goes on in this village, stays in this village."

"But don't you ever want to know the politics of the country and what is going to happen to Graceland?"

"Why? Whatever decisions they make out there does not affect us. We have our own government that governs our lives. The Chief is the one who makes the decisions and most of the time there is nothing for him to do except keep peace amongst the people. Anyone who is found making trouble is taken to him and the chief settles the problems. As for the city people, I don't think they can handle living this way of life. According to them, this is uncivilized."

"True, but don't people out here have to fight for their rights? Kind of like Ted Tembo, the father of the union."

"People out here don't know who Ted Tembo is. If he were to come out here, to them, he would only be a black man in white men's clothes. All they know is to survive and their only spokesperson is their Chief and his right hand men who are kind of like the members of parliament who don't really do anything, but sit there and look pretty." He joked.

"Will I get to meet the chief?"

"Sure, if you like. I don't see why not."
They continued talking about politics and Munique was impressed with how much the ten-year old knew about the government and the politics thatwere going on. When they reached the village, he let one of the men take Kungulu to meet the Chief while he waited with Catherine in a clearing by the hut.

"He is a very intelligent boy." he commented
"Yes, but I feel he needs to find his own place. Kungulu has had a hard time trying to fit in with the other children his age. I know that you are very busy, but could you help him bring back faith into his life? He seems to have lost it. I am afraid that one of these days his mother and I are going to lose him to retaliation."

"His mother?" Munique laughed to himself about what he had been thinking earlier on.

"What is so funny?"

"Oh, nothing. I thought he was your child."

"Oh no, no, no, no, no." She protested. "I love him like he is my own, but no, no, he is not mine." She imagined how her family would react if Kungulu was her child. She shook her head again and then laughed at the thought of seeing her parents' reaction if she were to announce to them that her child was half black. What a sight it would be.

"Haven't you ever thought about having a child of your own?"

"I have thought about it, yes. All women do. I hope to have one of my own someday. What about you? Don't you ever wish you could have children of your own?"

"Being a priest means making a lot of sacrifices."

"But have you ever thought about it?"

"Yes, I have, but working with children compensates for that. There is nothing better than to see a smile on a child who thought that they had almost lost everything."

"That is exactly how I feel about Gulu." "Why don't you come and work with me out here for a few weeks." He couldn't believe what he was asking her. It was a great risk he was taking to spend more time with her.

"I don't know I have a clinic to run."

"Don't you have another doctor there?"

"Yes, but . . ."

"Then it's settled. Besides, the women here like you and you seem to like it here yourself."

After a little bit more convincing, she smiled and nodded and agreed to do it. Gulu came out of the hut feeling enlightened and more up lifted. His face seemed to glow, like a prophet had inspired him. When Catherine asked him how it was, he could not stop talking about the great man he just spoke to. Kungulu described him as the Mahatma Ghandi of Africa. A wise man that had a philosophical answer to every question he had. When he had first entered the clay hut, he was afraid because it was dim and musty. The fat chief sturdily sat on a hand carved wooden chair with his hands resting on his knees and his body was draped with a white sheet that outlined his round belly. His deep dark complexion that was almost black made his eyes sparkle and perfect white teeth glow. The expression on his face was hard. This didn't scare Kungulu until he spoke out.

"Enjitaye." His voice was deep and rich. He signalled for Kungulu to sit down. "Don't you understand?" He said in perfect English. Kungulu shook his head slowly and knew better than to blink an eye in the presence of this noble man.

"You should learn to speak your mother's language. You cannot fo'get the little things that you are made of. Soon enough you will fo'get everything and you will disappear. Pa!" He slapped his hands together and made Kungulu jump. Startling the boy made him laugh. "You don't know who you are, do you?" Once again, Kungulu wondered how he knew how he was feeling. "Fighting with other people won't solve anything." After hearing that, Kungulu was convinced that this man could read his mind. I better watch what I am thinking or else he will read my mind again, he thought to himself.

"And then we talked about everything." All in one breath, he excitedly told Catherine everything they talked about. He finally thanked her with a tight hug around her hips. "Catty, thank you for bringing me here. Can we come again?"

"When we have time, yes." Munique admired the motherly expression in Catherine's face and felt a sudden flow of love for her overcome him.

Munique entered an old church in town and knelt down before another priest in a confessional cubical.

"Forgive me father for I have sinned."

"What have you done that has brought you here?"

Munique started to sweat and his hands got clammy.

"I have fallen in love with a woman, but I have already devoted myself to the church."

"I know." The priest answered. Munique looked hard at the shadow that was before him.

"Gunther, is that you?"

"Munique, would you feel more comfortable if we went somewhere else to talk?"

"Yes, yes, I think that would be good." He sighed feeling more comfortable. They walked out to the back of the church where they sat on a stone bench to talk.

"Now, tell me who this woman is."Munique explained to him how Catherine made him feel every hour and every minute of the day and how he felt guilty about it because he had already devoted himself to the church.

"Why are you feeling so guilty when you have not done anything? Falling in love with a woman does not mean that you are going to lose your faith in God. It only means that somebody else is giving you the loving feeling which you share with the rest of the world."

"I never thought of it like that. But it has gotten to the extent that I cannot resist the temptation to..."

"Have sex with the woman, yes, yes, I know." He finished the sentence for him. "You must learn to resist the temptation. I was in love once, but I was young. She was everything I thought I wanted."

"But she is what I want. Don't you see? I have turned my back on God....."

"Munique, answer me honestly. Do you think you are ready to leave the church to become a part of this woman's life?" There was a sudden pause when Munique held his breath in before he could answer. He knew he could not lie.

"Yes."

"Have you thought about this? I mean really thought about it."

"I have thought about it until I turned blue."

"It seems to me that you have already made up your mind. I don't see why you came here anyway."

"I just wanted to be sure, and I also needed to tell someone about it."

"You shouldn't be telling me about it. Tell her."

"I don't know how. I have never been in this situation before. I have never been with a woman before either. I wouldn't know how to approach her."

"Listen to me. You will know when the time is right. Just like when you were ready to devote yourself to the church. For the longest time I have known you, you have been the most dedicated man to the Catholic Church. You know as much as I know that you cannot have the best of both worlds. How does she feel about you leaving the church?"

"She doesn't know yet. She doesn't even know how I really feel about her."

"Well you better tell her before you give up what you have worked for so many years. She may be someone who may not even care about you." They talked for another hour about his situation and prayed together as brothers. Munique decided that he was going to go on with his life until he was certain about the way Catherine felt about him.

Chapter Three

1969.

"**B**oys! Boys! Stop this instant!" A nun in a white vale pushed her way through the jeering crowd of boys who crowded around a fight. She pushed them away and grabbed the two ten year old boys who were rumbling in a cloud of dust. The cheering stopped and the nun dismissed the other children once she grabbed hold of the two boys. "As for you two, it is off to the Head Master's office."

"But Sister, Peter started it!"

"Matthew, I don't want to hear it. Save your story for Mr Dugans." She dragged the boys by their ears all the way into the Head Master's office.

The two boys stood there with their heads hung low, looking at the floor. Mr Dugans, a well respected man, towered the boys in his black robe with his arms crossed. He was a man of great prestige and many praised him for the work he did in the school. In the twelve years he had been Head Master at the Little Angels, he was able to put the two segregated schools into one without any protesters violating the district. He had received some personal threats at home, but nothing serious was ever done to his family. The government and the people had grown to accept the Little Angels as an up graded school which helped bring peace amongst the white and black Gracelanders. On the outside, he exposed himself as a man who strived for unification, but on the inside, he spent sleepless nights worried about his family who suffered for his cause. With their heads hung low, the boys did not dare move or make a sound. They continued to look at the floor as they waited for their punishment.

"Mr Peter Setaro, you may leave." He said calmly.

"Yes, sa." The little black boy's voice was small and timid. He darted for the door before Mr Dugans could change his mind.

"Now, Mr Zulu. What have you got to say for yourself?" He paced before the coloured boy and waited for him to say something. "Well?"

"He called me a white-nigger bastard, sa."

"Because he called you a name you chose to hit him?"

Kungulu did not answer, but only kept on looking at the floor. Mr Dugans knelt down before him and levelled his eyes with him and calmly continued.

"Don't be afraid. Look at me when I am talking to you, Matthew." The boy raised his head and looked straight into Mr Dugans' grey eyes.

"That is better." he added and sounded more reassuring. "This is the third school your mother has sent you to in the past two years. You have only been here for three weeks and you have already been in four fights. Matthew, I know that you are a good student. Your teacher tells me you have very good marks and you work very hard. Is there something troubling you at home that you want me to know about? I am here to help you."

Silence.

The child's expression was ice cold.He stood there frowning with his lips perked tightlyand without fear; he looked deep into Mr Dugans'eyes. Stubborn child, thought Mr Dugans. This was going to be a tough one to break into.

"I'll tell you what, Matthew,"

"Kungulu." He interjected.

"What?"

"My name is Kungulu."

"You know the rules. You use your Christened name at school and your African name at home. Isn't your Christened name Matthew?"

"No. My mother only gave me one name. Kungulu."

"I see." The Head Master rose to his feet and walked behind his desk and grabbed a cane which lay on the window sill. "You know what Matthew?"

"Kungulu."

"Matthew." He stressed. For the first time in his career, Mr Dugans was losing his patience with a student. "I am not like other teachers or other Head Masters you have had and I promise you, I will teach you to have some respect for elders and I will also teach you to not fight on my school grounds. Now, turn around and let this be a lesson to you."

"No."

"Do as I say or you will really get what you deserve."

"My own mother doesn't beat me with a cane and you want to beat me? No."

"My patience is running out Matthew!"

"Kungulu!" He shouted back.

"Turn around!"

"No!" He grabbed the boy by the arm, turned him around and started beating his back side with the cane. Kungulu did not scream, cry or shout. He held his breath and waited until it was over.

Kungulu quietly walked into the kitchen from the back door and his mother instantly knew that he had gotten into another fight at school.

"You got into another fight, didn't you? How many times do I have to tell you not to fight? I am tired of this! Go have a wash and go to bed. No supper fo' you. Well, what are you standing around he'e fo'. Go, go! Out!" She waved her hand at him and shooed him away like a fly. He walked out with his head hung low, and his books in one hand. When he got to their quarters, he carefully washed himself and tried to avoid touching his back side. The cold water soothed the pain, but it was only for a while. He got dressed and climbed into bed and lay on his stomach and tried not to move until his mother came in a few hours later.

"Get up and eat." She sat next to him on the side of the bed with a plate of food in her lap.

"But I thought you said,..."

"Neva mind what I said. No son of mine is going to sta've, now eat."

He tried to roll over to his side, but the pain was too much.

"I can't." The tears flooded his eyes as he began to cry hysterically.

"What's the matter? Gulu?"

"Mama," he sobbed

"Gulu, what's wrong?" She rested her hand on his back side and he flinched. She peeled away the sheets and his night clothes and saw that his back was swollen with black and blue bruises between his waist and his thighs.

"Who did this to you?"

"Mr Dugans."

"Ms Zulu, you can't go in there!" The secretary ran after Sarah who had already barged into Mr Dugans' office. When she walked in, Mr Dugans was having a meeting with two white parents. He sat behind his desk with his hands clasped looking as professional as ever. Once he saw her walk into his office with her head held high, her dress neatly pressed along her pleats, and her hat placed carefully on her head, he stood up from his seat.

"I have come to talk to you about my son, Mr Dugans." She said firmly.

"I am in a meeting, and if you could so kindly wait outside I will, . . ."

"I will not talk later; I will talk with you now. My son is a very serious matter." The white couple glanced at the two parties who glared at each other, and they felt the tension grow in the room. "Or would you like for me to tell these lovely parents what you did to my son. Hm?"

At that moment, he hated her for embarrassing him in front of other people. He was a well respected man who did not need such exposure from a woman who did not mean anything to him. He carefully turned his attention to the white couple and apologized for ending the meeting early and asked them to come in tomorrow. Once they left, his expression changed.

"In all my years at the Little Angels, I have never had a parent complain about the way I treat the students."

"Well, Mr Dugans, there is always a first time for everything."

"I gave your son the same treatment I give children who need to be disciplined."

"My son came home battered and bruised. In my book that's abuse, not discipline. As his mother, I have never beaten my son. Just because other children don't accept him for the person he is, it doesn't mean that he has to be punished fo' it. As a single mother I can only afford to give him the love and the security he needs. Don't make his life any more difficult than it is. What made you think you had the right to beat him like an animal? He is a child, Mr Dugans. My child, not yours. If you ever lay another hand on my son, may God help you, because I will come after you with my own bare hands."

She started to walk out the door, and as she gripped the door handle, she turned around and then added,

"Actually, I don't want my son around you or your institution. I am withdrawing him from your school. Good day." She turned her back to him and walked out the door and down the corridor. The secretary and Mr Dugans looked on after her.

"Now we know where Matthew gets his attitude from," said the secretary.

"Kungulu." Sarah interjected.

"What?" Mr Dugans asked confused.

"The boy's name is Kungulu." He said, and walked back into his office and closed the door behind him.

From that day on, Kungulu started taking private lessons with Catherine. She taught him things from mathematics to French and Afrikaans. One of the most important things which she tried to do was encourage him to read. It was not as difficult as she thought it would be. The ten year old enjoyed reading whatever he could get his hands on including newspapers and magazines. One day she even found him reading one of her romance novels which she had to confiscate and hide out of sight along with the rest of her collection.

On the other hand, it worried Sarah that he was not associating with any of the other children. She noticed that he never went outside to play with the other children. Kungulu had a hard time trying to fit in with the other children. The black children accepted him more than the white children, but they were both equally prejudiced. His light complexion and sandy kinky brown hair made him stand out from the others. Every time they played football or cricket, he was always the last one to be picked.

There was one other little girl who was half black and half white who Kungulu grew attached to. They never had to say much to each other except hold hands and give each other a smile. Kungulu knew that she understood him because she was just like him, but more beautiful. She had big green eyes and long thick curly hair which was always tied in braided pig tails down to her shoulders. Camellia was only five when they met and she loved Kungulu because he always told her stories and read her fairy tales under a large tree near the lake where fishermen occasionally floated their boats on the calm water surface. She explained to Kungulu that Cinderella was her favourite because it reminded her of herself. She was the poor little girl who was still waiting for her Godmother to come and grant her the wish to escape the traitorous world and one day, everybody who was mean to her, including her father, would bow down before her and they would become her servants. Kungulu only told her that she was crazy because the government would never let coloured girls become rulers of a country. It was the law.

Kungulu had learned a lot about politics from just reading the papers. Although he didn'tunderstand most of what was being said, he had anidea of what was going on in his own country as wellas other places. He never stopped asking Catherinequestions about what a System of Proclamation wasor what White Supremacy meant. One thing whichhe grew to realize was that he did not fit in anycategory. He was neither black nor white. He was coloured. It was ironic to be an individual especiallywhen he was a combination of both races which wereat war with each other. He was determined to findhis own crowd which accepted him in his owncountry. He read the paper every day and listened tothe news and found nothing about coloureds.

When he turned twelve, he was more aware of the fact that there were more coloureds living in Graceland, but they lived in their own community a few hundred miles near Takoma City at the coastal region at a place called Makala. They were middle class people who had their own businesses and lifestyle which were not associated with the black and white colonies. They lived their own lives and created their own mandate which kept the racist world outside the walls of their community. Kungulu wanted to go and visit Makala and see these people and see whether they would understand him and maybe they would be blind to his appearance and whetherthey could see through the window in his heart. Forthe meantime, he had to live in a world where his mother, Cathy and his friend Camellia really accepted him. One day he had then turned to his mother and mentioned to her that everyone else had somebody fighting their wars for them, but who was going to fight the war for him? She kindly said to him in a motherly voice,

"I will," she said cunningly "and anyone else who loves you will always fight fo' you." Yes, it was comforting to hear, but he wanted to hear something else. He wanted to hear more than the loving words from his mother. Even the Bellmonts, who grew to like him as one of their own, gave him the attention he needed, especially Mr Bellmont. At first he found Gulu to be a nuisance until one day he saw him reading his paper. They hit it off quite well when they both agreed that the South African cricket team was better than the British. Mr Bellmont even took him to watch a cricket match with him and proudly introduced him to some of his colleagues. They talked about how their national team could be stronger if all the best players of the white and black teams could come together and form a team. Like in all social events, Kungulu was able to take part in the political discussions amongst Mr Bellmont's colleagues. Mr Bellmont watched and admired him from a distance and found himself being absorbed in the child's presence. Gulu became the son he never had. He started to teach him all the things he knew and encouraged him to never stop learning. When Kungulu walked alongside him, he tried to imitate Mr Bellmont's actions and quickly picked up on his speech and expressions which Mr Bellmont found intriguing to see his little shadow follow through his footsteps.

Kungulu enjoyed spending time with Mr Bellmont, but it wasn't the same as spending time with Camellia. She was different in a nice kind of way. He didn't understand why other children never liked her. Maybe they were jealous of her because she could pass for being white and could get away with having more privileges than they did. She never bothered anyone and never said anything to anyone or about anyone. She even told Kungulu that even her own parents didn't love her and all they did was beat her and scream at her even when she didn't do anything wrong.

She never did say much about her parents. All Kungulu knew was that she lived on Mr William Jones' farm, a man who kept to himself most of the time. He never associated with anyone unless it was business. Then there were also rumours about him keeping slaves on his farm. Kungulu suspected that he was her father because   he   was   the   only   white   man on the farm.

Kungulu had to find out the truth for himself so one day, so he decided to go pay Camellia a visit. He walked through the rusted black gates of Mr Jones' estate and all the way up to the wooden porch. The black servants around the yard watched him to see what he was going to do next. Kungulu knocked on the door three times and one of the men stepped up to him and said,

"Are you mad? If you had any brains you wouldn't come he'e at all. Now go. Go befo'e he sees you." Just as he started dragging him by the arm, a black woman with a white apron answered the door. She looked at him wide eyed with a sense of fear lingering in her face.

"I came to see Camellia, is she in?"

"No." She answered quickly, and with hesitation she added, "You must be Gulu. She talks about you all the time." Her dried cracked lips almost gave a smile until someone yelled from inside the house.

"Toni! Tonjeli, who is at the door?"

"Nobody!" She yelled back. She took Kungulu's hand in her trembling bony ones and said, "you betta go chil'. This no place fo' you. I tell Camellia you look fo' ha."

Before Kungulu could even start walking away, Camellia flew through the door with her dress half undone. She clung to Kungulu's arm almost digging her nails into his skin.

"Camellia, come back here. I am not finished with you yet!" A shabby middle aged man with his shirt unbuttoned revealing his hairy beer belly with his suspender straps hanging from his sides, staggered out the front door.

Camellia pulled Kungulu's arm and the next thing he knew, they were running out the gate and down the dusty road. They arrived at a tree near the lake where they sat to catch their breaths. As they leaned against the tree, Kungulu noticed that her legs and bare feet were covered with blood.

"Camellia, you are bleeding."

"Gulu," she choked on her words and tried to cry, but she couldn't. "He hurt me. He cut me and hurt me again and again and again." Her body trembled as she tightly wrapped her arms around his neck.

He helped her to the side of the lake to wash the blood off of her legs and inner thighs, but it was useless. The blood kept flowing from between her legs and they didn't know how to stop it. When he saw that she was losing colour in her face, he half carried her back to his house and hid her in the garden shed and went to get Catherine from the main house.

"Cathy, can you keep a secret?"

"Of course, you know you can trust me."

"Camellia is hurt and she needs a doctor, but I can't take her back to her house."

"Where is she?"

"She is in the shed in the yard. But you have to promise not to tell anyone where she is."

"Gulu, if she is hurt, she needs help." When Catherine saw the little girl lying unconscious on the moulding wooden floor of the tool shed, she bent down to feel her pulse. The moment she felt something, she picked her up, rushed over to her jeep and put her in the passenger seat.

"Gulu, get in. We are taking her to the hospital."

"But you promised you wouldn't let anyone know where she was."

"Gulu, if we don't get her to the hospital she will die! Now, get in the car."

The thought of losing his best friend made his eyes redden and fill with tears. He held her close to him until they got to the hospital where she was rushed into the emergency room to be examined by two doctors and a nurse.

The time that past seemed like hours before one of the doctors approach Catherine to tell her that Camellia's condition was critical and that she needed to stay overnight in the hospital so that more tests could be done. Then the doctor stated that she had been physically and sexually abused a number of times. By looking at the old scars, bruises and cigarette burns, it had been going for a period of time. If they hadn't brought her in, she could have died from haemorrhaging. Her vagina had been sliced about an inch with a blunt object and there were also signs of penetration. Because she had been beaten so many times, there was a ninety per cent chance that she would not be able to have children once she reached puberty. The doctor also said that she had to be treated for an infection which was spreading in her uterus which was probably caused by unsanitary objects which might have been inserted into her vagina.

"Of course miracles do happen, but we have to be prepared for the worst. We have many of these cases every day and sometimes children younger than her don't survive. She is very lucky. She is a strong girl.

She will pull through." On that last note, the doctor looked at his clipboard and glanced at his watch before he went to tend to another patient. Catherine tried to fight back the tears before she turned to talk to Kungulu who helplessly sat in the waiting room. When he saw her walk towards him, he jumped up from his seat and said eagerly,

"Is she okay? Can I go see her? What did the doctor say?"

"Gulu," she swallowed hard and tried to find the words to tell him how she was doing. She bent down, levelled her eyes with his and tried to explain to him the best she could. "Sweetness, Camellia is very ill and she has to stay in the hospital tonight, but the doctor said that she is going to be all right."

"Can I go see her?"

"Only for a little while because she is sleeping." A lump formed in her throat when she saw the desolate look on Kungulu's face. She took him by the hand and led him into Camellia's room where two other women also lay helpless in the beds next to hers. The room was dim and the two fans which swirled quietly above their heads only circulated the antiseptic aroma that lingered in the air. Kungulu went to Camellia's bedside and looked at her pale face which was motionless. He lightly touched her forehead with his finger tips and his eyes flooded with tears. He sniffed and kissed her gently on the temple. He didn't know what to say, except stand there and stare at her and hope for her to open her eyes, or give him a small smile. Maybe just a twitch. Something. Anything. Anything to let him know that she was getting better. Instead, she lay quietly and motionless with her eyes closed on the starched white sheets.

Catherine entered Mr Jones' yard and aggressively banged on his door three times with her fist and tried to lurk through the screen door. The timid and frightened servants stood and watched her like curious pathetic forest animals afraid to approach her. None of them dare question or step up to the white woman who had a temper in her voice like their master's.

"Mr Jones, I have come to see you about Camellia!" She yelled through the screen door. She heard rustling followed by footsteps. Catherine tried to look through the screen to see the person who was approaching the door. He slowly opened the door enough for her to see his face.

"Mr Jones, I have come to tell you that your daughter is in hospital."

"Why? She wasn't sick. What's wrong with her?"

"She is very ill; Mr Jones and you are the cause of it. I know exactly what you have been up to and what sort of farm you run here.

"What are you talking about?"

"You know very well what I am talking about, sir. You make me sick, molesting and raping your own daughter? If I were you I would get a lawyer, because charges are being brought up against you for what you have been doing to her."

"You wouldn't do that."

"Watch me."

"Look, the relationship between my family members is none of your business or the court's. As her father, I have every right to raise her however way I like. Besides, the law cannot interfere with family affairs. You have no case Miss . . . whoever you are."

"You ignorant mole, where have you been? Little

do you know what types of charges could be brought up against you. May I remind you that I am aware of the fact that you don't pay your employees for their labour. May I remind you, slavery was abolished over fifty years ago. Get out of your hole and see what is around you."

"Get off my land, bitch." She could smell the liquor on his breath as he spat the words at her. "If you want to talk about the law, then may I remind you that I have the right to shoot you for trespassing on my property? Now bugger off before I put a bullet through your head. Get!" She stepped back when he stepped up to her with his body only inches away from hers.

"Order in court!" Voices quieted down. "Please rise."

The white judge walked into the court with his black robe and white wig. Everyone sat down after he pulled his chair in and wiped his moon glasses. The court room was now quiet except for the shuffling of people getting comfortable in the court and an occasional cough in the right corner of the room. The two fans on the high ceiling whirled and only circulated the stuffy air and the smell of the sweating bodies.

Camellia sat next to a middle aged woman lawyer that Catherine had appointed to protect her. Camellia turned around to face Catherine and Gulu who were sitting right behind her. Catherine smiled and nodded her head to let her know that they are there for her and that they wouldn't be going anywhere. Catherine looked around her as she anxiously waited for Sarah to walk through the courtroom doors. Instead, Father Munique walked through the doors dressed in his priest robe. She was surprised to see him. He hadn't seen her. She turned back around and put her arm around Gulu. Camellia took a deep breath and felt more comfortable to know that her supporters were nearby. At that moment, she saw her father walk through the doors and was looking straight at her. He did not take his eyes off her until he sat down with his lawyer at a table across from where she was sitting. The judge glanced at the papers on his desk through his half mooned glasses and lazily started to state his evaluation.

"Will the defendant please stand." Mr Jones stood up and buttoned his suit jacket and touched his tie to make sure it was in place. He looked like a totally different man with his shaven face and neatly combed hair. Surprisingly, he looked dignified in the eyes of the court."

Now Mr Jones, you have been charged with sexual and physical abuse upon your own daughter Camellia Jones. Is that right?"

"Yes, your honour."

"And how do you plea?"

"Not guilty."

"Be seated."

The judge looked over his half-mooned glasses at Camellia and her lawyer. "Ms Kapepe, please call your first witness." The young black lawyer in her long black dress stood up and called for Camellia's mother to take the stand.

The fragile woman walked up to the stand with her head hung low dressed in a colourful printed shirt and matching skirt with a black head dress neatly wrapped around her head. She sat down and stated her name coyly.

"Tonjeli. Tonjeli Jones." The court could hear the nervousness in her voice, but they couldn't see her sweating palms that she rubbed together in her lap. Ms Kapepe stepped away from her table and approached Mrs Jones at the witness stand. For a black lawyer, she had won ten large cases that attracted the media in the three years that she had been a lawyer. For not only being a black lawyer, but also a woman, to be capable of winning cases for blacks who were on trial, was an outstanding record. At times she would even take cases for free depending on the condition and the charges brought up against the individual.

Susan Kapepe was educated in the United States by her great uncle who was a lawyer. She learned all that she needed to know about American law, and when she moved back home to Graceland, she started studying law under the British Government. She knew as much as any good lawyer would have to know about law, but because she was black and a woman, she was not licensed to practice law. She fought her way to the top and won her case under Article Six paragraph nine, this does not only abolish slavery, but also gives every individual the right to work and serve their country as they wish. The Article, "No one shall be enslaved by another . . . and equal rights to work and serve the country should be granted to all," was what won her case. The law did not exclude women or children, therefore, she won the case and had the privilege to work as a lawyer and serve her country and her people. The only thing that prevented her from winning most of her cases were prejudice judges.

Her heels echoed across the wooden floor of the courtroom as she proceeded on asking the witness her questions.

"Mrs Jones, is that your daughter over there?"

"Yes." She looked at her daughter warmly as she answered the question moderately.

"Please speak up so the court can hear you."

"Yes, she my daughter." She spoke out louder and in a stronger accent.

"Mrs Jones, who is that man?" She pointed to Mr Jones who sat in front of her.

"My husband."

"Are you sure?"

"Yes."

"When did you get married?"

"We never had a wedding."

"Is there any official document that states that you are husband and wife?" Tonjeli looked around her with eyes wide and Ms Kapepe could see the sweat glistening above her lip.

"I don't know. He took me from owa village after my mother and father die and he say he would marry me and take care of me."

"So, you don't know whether there is any official documentation that states whether you are husband and wife?"

"No."

"Have you ever seen your husband, or should I say, your significant other, hit or sexually violate your daughter?"

Tonjeli looked at her husband feeling frightened for her life as well as her daughter's. She lingered on that question and hesitated to answer. Ms Kapepe approached the witness stand and reassured her that nobody was going to hurt her if she truthfully answered the question.

"It's going to be all right. Please answer the question."

She looked down at her hands and shook her head. The Judge was losing his patience with her spending so much time to answer a simple question and feeling irritated, he said,

"Please answer yes or no Mrs Jones. We haven't got all day."

"No, Sa."

"Mrs Jones, are you sure that your husband has never laid a hand on your daughter?"

"Yes."

"Mrs Jones, do you know what the penalty for lying on the witness stand while under oath is?"

"Objection your honour, the witness has already answered the question and she perfectly knows that she is under oath."

"Sustained."

"But your honour, the woman is ignorant to the rules of the court room and I feel she should be aware of the consequences of not telling the truth while on the witness stand."

"Well she should have thought about it before she took the stand. Now carry on, or don't you have any more questions?"

Ms Kapepe knew that this trial was not going to be easy. Tonjeli was too frightened to tell the truth. Who wouldn't be of a man who practically controlled her life and determined whether she lived or died? Either way, Ms Kapepe continued on with the trial for the next few hours. All the witnesses who took the stand, including Mr Jones' gardener, cook, and even a few of the field workers, denied the fact that Mr Jones was a violent man. The gardener who had a scar that ran from his ear to his cheek bone denied that he had been beaten or whipped by Mr Jones, and instead lied and said he had tripped over his panga. Kapepe knew she had lost the case.

Mr Jones must have threatened every single one of them if they told the truth. There was nothing that she could do for the little girl now.

Evidently, Ms Kapepe lost the trial. The Judge dismissed the charges on Mr Jones on the lack of evidence and witnesses, and Camellia was to return in his custody.

When it was all over, everyone in the courtroom started filling out the door and were commenting on the verdict.

"Cathy, what does that mean? What does that mean, Cathy?" Gulu tugged at the sleeve of her dress as he tried to get her attention. She leaned down to him and spoke softly. Father Munique noticed her when she caught his eye, smiled, and quickly looked away. He tried to catch up to her, but she was gone before he could get a chance to speak to her.

As time passed after the trial, Kungulu never saw Camellia again. His thirteenth birthday came and went and there was still no sign of Camellia. She had not been to school in months and other children who didn't care for her, started noticing her absence. Day after day, Kungulu would go to the big tree near the lake where he had hoped she would come by or stop to rest for a while, but she never came. Whenever he had the chance, he would go by her father's farm and from behind a bush. He would hide and wait to see if he could get a glimpse of her in the yard. He never saw her. She was nowhere to be seen. When the winter season came and went, he stopped going to the lake and chose to put the past behind him as his mother had suggested. He never talked of Camellia again and forced himself to suppress his memories of her and the trial. It was too painful for him to remember everything.

Chapter Four

1971.

It was a little before eight in the morning when Catherine pulled up into the drive way of her clinic. FatherMunique sat on her front steps with his leather hat shieldinghis face from the morning sun.

"Good morning, father. What brings you here this early in the morning?"

When he got up to make room for her to open the front door, he removed his hat and rotated the rim of it withthe tips of his fingers.

"Good morning Miss Bellmont..."

"Catherine, please. Why are you being formal withme?"

"Catherine," he repeated after her and then followedbehind her into her office. "I would like you to come down to our parish and take a look at our mare. She hasn'tbeen eating very much lately and has been very sluggish. I am not sure whether she has a fever or not."

"I will come down with you, but I can't leave until myassistant gets in this morning. Do you mind waiting?"

"No, of course not." He comfortably sat in one of thetwo chairs in front of her desk.

"Cup of tea?"

"Yes, please."

Once she served the tea, Father Munique felt nervous.Why was he feeling nervous around her? He watched herevery move, even when she carefully took a sip out of hercup, it made him smile. This is a woman with a lot ofcharacter, he thought. At that moment, the front door opened.

"Morning Cat!"

"I am in the office!" She yelled back. Charlie walkedinto her office not realizing that she was not alone.

"Sorry, I didn't know that you were busy."

"No, no, come on in." She insisted.

"Please don't get up." He told Father Munique as heshook his hand. "I just wanted to come and see how my sisteris doing. He crossed over to her and gave her a kiss.

"This early in the morning?" She frowned suspiciously.

"Well, I have some business to take care of this morning and I thought I would take some time out to see you." He reached for her cup and took a sip almost burnt histongue. "There are never enough hours in the day." He complained.

"I know what you mean." Father Munique agreed.

"What kind of business are you in?" Charlie asked.

"He is a priest." Catherine quickly answered for him.

"Oh. You sure don't look like one. I mean, you're wearing jeans and a casual shirt, and the priests I have seenaround these parts are always in black and wear a white collar. I am sure it must get kind of hot underneath all that black clothing and ring around your collar....It has been years since I went to confession," he rambled, "If I were to go now, the poor priest would probably die from exhaustion after listening to all the sins I have

committed." He took another sip from her cup and added as he started for the door, "I don't
know how you can drink this without any sugar. Well, got torun. Pleasure meeting you Father, and I will see you later Cat.

Bye!" and he was gone before they could even answer him.

"That is my baby brother for you." she apologisedwith a tint of red in her cheeks.
Once her assistant arrived, they were off to the parish.
Father Munique watched her examine the horse. She finally concluded that the horse was pregnant and her sluggishness was due to being over worked. From that day on, FatherMunique found every excuse to see Catherine. From lamegoats to stray dogs, Father Munique brought them toCatherine to examine. He loved to see her work with herhands and when she did smile, her face glowed. Just seeingher always made him feel whole hearted and complete.

Each time he saw her, he always felt the need to embrace her, hold her, and love her. When he did, it onlyhappened once and he promised himself that he would not letit happened again. He was on his way out of her office oneday when they kissed. The moment seemed so right and soperfect. It made him feel warm on the inside and with hisarms wrapped around her; he could feel her heart beat againsthis. Was it just him, or did she feel it too? This feeling frightened him. To resist the temptation, he vowed not to seeher anymore.
For the next three weeks, he spent most of his time
working around the parish handling confessions, preaching, and helping around the little orphanage they were running.

With the rest of his free time, he avoided going into town andchose to stay in closed doors and pray.

97

The other priests wondered why he, the most prominent community oriented priest of them all, stopped going out to spread the word of the Lord. They prayed for him and hoped that whatever illness hehad, he was going to overcome it. Even he himself prayedendlessly and on occasions fell asleep with the bible in hishands.

Wednesday afternoon seemed to drag on forever as hesat in the booth listening to people's confessions. As the nextperson entered the booth, he started again,"In the name of the Father and of the Son, and of theHoly Spirit, Amen." he said through the curtain to the figureon the other side.

"Forgive me Father, for I have sinned."

"When was the last time you went to confession?"

"Oh, I don't know. It's been years."He recognized the voice and held his breath in. When
he did not answer, the voice continued,

"Father, I don't know whether it is a sin, but I havefallen in love with a man, not any man, but a priest. He is everything that I have ever wanted. He is gentle, kind, caring, loving... and I miss him." She spoke softly, almost in awhisper.

"He is only doing his job as a priest to spread the love of God."
"I understand that he has duties to the church, but for myself, I want to know how he feels about me. Munique, why did you run off like that?" He took a moment before heanswered.

"As a priest I am married to the church and my devotion lies upon serving the Lord."

"But as a man, how do you feel?" She insisted.
"As a man... I love you more than you can imagine, but I am a priest and,"

"I know! All my life I have been afraid and angry atthe world. You made me feel safe and see the world differently. I don't want to lose you, Munique. When you stopped coming to see me, I thought it was something that Isaid or did."

"Catherine, it is best you don't come here. I need tobe alone. Please. In the name of the Father, and of the Son, and of the Holy Spirit, Amen." He quickly got up and walkedout of the booth.

"Munique," her voice echoed in the empty church asshe followed on behind him. He turned around and could seethe despair in her eyes and hated himself for that. She knewthat there was nothing else she could do. "I'm sorry. I didn't mean to cause any problems. They do say that if you lovesomeone, set them free..." She swallowed hard and her eyesfilled with tears. Before she turned to leave, she kissed himon the cheek and felt her heart sink to her feet. "Good-bye, Father."

After she left, he sat in the church thinking and praying hard with his hands clasped tightly together.

"Please God, help me, and give me a sign, anything. I don't know what to do." He pleaded to Jesus on the wooden cross that hung solemnly above the alter. He glanced around him and studied the walls of the house of the Lord. There wasa marble statue of the Virgin Mary with her head facing theearth and her palms open before her. There was a series ofpaintings of Jesus carrying the cross, Jesus being nailed to the cross, Jesus hanging from the cross, Jesus showing his wounds to his disciples after resurrecting from the dead, and Jesus ascending into heaven with angels around him gloriously singing and glowing graciously. The church walls stared back at him and circled through his mind. He closedhis eyes and pleaded to God for an answer.

But he could still feel her lips against his from the lasttime they kissed in her office. Her lips were so sweet, so soft, and so tender. He bit his bottom lip and looked up at the cross one more time. He made the sign of the cross and left the church.

Johnny's back hand with the jagged ring came flying across the man's face making his lip bleed.

"Don't you ever try to steal from me again. Next timeI will cut your hand off and feed it to the dogs. You remember now that you work for me. If you mess up again, it will be your head. No, even better, your family. I hear youhave a very pretty wife, eh?"
The man's eyes grew wide in fear of what Johnny was capable of doing to him and his family.

"Okay, okay," the man stammered. "I will bring backtwice as much next time, but please, don't hurt my family.

"Then you better behave. Now listen to me. There ismore work for you to do. Go to Kenjezi Mines and find outhow much gold they are mining each day. I will give you twodays and no more. For each day that you are late, I will cut afinger off your wife's hand. Now, get out of he'e."

The man scrambled to his feet and walked passedJohnny with his head hung low.

"I tell you Charlie, these nigge's need to be talked tolike children. It is the only way they will understand what we are saying." Charlie lit his cigar and stood up from his chair.

"You can't complain Johnny, we have a 23% profitin the past year and if we want to keep that stable, we have toslow the operation down now that the Allied

100

Union Workersis growing. In six months Teddy Tembo has been able toenrol ten thousand people and I don't think he has anyintentions of stopping there."

"The Union and Tembo. Agh! What can they do? March outside owa office with their 'Stop Manual Labour'signs?"

"Johnny, you've got to be realistic. Things are changing and they are getting kind of rough these days. Nowit is 'power to the people' and 'down with white supremacy.'The other day I read in the paper that they were trying to passa "civilized labour policy" where whites could do menial labouralongside the blacks. They think that by trying to make thetitle sound more sophisticated things will be better, when infact what they are saying is that the civilized race will beslaving away alongside the blacks. What a contradiction. In the past five years the government has passed more Bills in favour of the blackies and sooner or later we may findourselves in jail for what we have been doing."

"Well, not necessarily."

"What do you mean?"

"Well, we could concentrate on blackmailing the village boys or we could just take their women and use them to our advantage,... if you know what I mean. We could setup a little hotel with all kinds of girls. Black, white, coloured, Indian, you name it, we will have it. That is another way of making money."

"No, no, Johnny. That operation is too risky. The Mutoto wa Mutoto is not what it is turning out to be. Our jobis to steal from other mines and I am not going to stoop solow as becoming a pimp. We have to change the wholesystem. There is too much at risk. Remember a few yearsago when that one lad from the Kukui Tribe managed to runaway? They almost traced him back to us."

"Oh, him."

"That was kind of rough wasn't it? The bastard couldn't tell the difference between a chisel and a hammer."

Charlie took another drag from his cigar and let the smokelinger around his face. "Useless." He thought out loud.

"Besides, I am tired of running after those ignorant fools whokeep slipping through our fingers. It is too much of a hassle."

They were quiet for a while as they both contemplated on what to do next, until Charlie started up theconversation again.

"I was thinking," He rose from his seat and took a fewpaces on the wooden floor as he pensively held his cigarbetween his fingers. "What about prisoners?"

"What about them? They practically have nothing tolive for anyway. Besides, half of them have lost their minds from being tortured by the police. Just come with me and Iwill show you what I mean. This may be the answer to all of our problems. Think about it. A man has a prison record. If he is caught stealing from mines, he will automatically bethrown back in jail and no further questioning will be madeand the tracks would be buried and nothing will be led back tous."

"I don't know. What about the bail fee? Won't theywonder why we would pay for his bail fee?"

"We won't have to. Trust me, this one is on me."

Kungulu tried to squeeze his way up to the front to hear Mr Tembo, a black politician and Freedom Fighter, speak for the Africans. His mother lingered in the back of the crowd as her heart pounded with excitement to hear the man who she had heard so much about.

"We, the *real* people of Africa, need our equal rights. Elections are coming and we don't even have the right to voteor even stand for elections! There is no one to represent usand answer to our needs. All we are asking for is one vote, one nation, and one people, to build our country. We welcomed the Europeans into our homes where they ate our bread and drank our water. In return they gave us slavery, poverty and suffering. We cried for freedom but they didn't hear us. They raped our women who screamed for mercy, butthey chose to not hear them. Maybe we should shout loud enough for them to hear us!" The crowd cheered and encouraged their leader to continue. "We want our voices
to be heard and our hearts and minds to be set free from theenslaving white government." The crowd roared, whistled and praised Tembo on with their hands waving in the air.

"They said they gave us the right to own land, but we became slaves in our own lands. They said they would show us theway to life, but they only showed us to our graves. They said they would give us equality, but they only gave us poverty.All of these are promises which they have failed to keep.

"I stand here before you as your brother, a union worker, a friend, and black freedom fighter. I am not, andneither are you, a bloody nigger bastard. I am a man ofdestiny as you are the real people of Africa who want to findyour own destiny to freedom.

"We should educate our children and remind them ofwho they are. When you tell them that they are black, they are Africans, not niggers. Their blood is as pure as the blacksoil that brings fruit to our earth. Teach them well to neverforget their heritage. Teach them well to never forget who they are and what being black really means.

You, as mothers and fathers, brothers and sisters, should say to yourselves, as I say to myself, no man shall step in my path to freedom. No one shall bury my tracks which Ihave made to fight back my own land and my own soul. VivaAfrica! Viva Mtesa! Give back owa country and owa people.Viva! Viva!" He clenched his right fist and held it highabove his head as the crowd did the same and cheered on'Viva Africa' and 'Viva Mtesa.'Meanwhile, white police officers with clubs pushedtheir way through the crowd towards the wooden platform andstood in front of the people holding onto their clubs tightlyand watching all the people gearing on louder and louder.

"Go home, all of you! You do not have a permit togather here." demanded the Commander in charge. When thepeople ignored him and continued to raise their fists abovetheir heads in sequence, their chants got louder and theCommander tried to get their attention until his face turnedred from yelling. He finally blew his whistle and climbed upon the platform.

"Please, go home. If you don't do as you are told, wewould have to force you out of here. We don't want anytrouble now. Go home."

"Ah, shut up you bloody honky. We have had enough!" yelled a man in the crowd. Other people aroundhim encouraged him and yelled back at the police officers.Some of them even spat at the officers' feet and continuedchanting.

"I won't ask you again!" The officer warned.

"We have a right to be here as much as you do." confirmed Tembo.

"Tell your people to go home or we will have to arrestthem. They are disturbing the peace and if you are notcareful, I will arrest you for encouraging a riot and disobeyingan officer."

"I have as much right as you do to be here," he replied coolly. The Commander pushed Tembo to indicatehim to leave. The crowd got restless when they saw theofficer push their successor. They tried to push their waythrough to the top of the platform, but the police standingbefore them started clubbing them on their heads. The crowdbecame wild with rage. The screams were a combination ofanger amongst the men, and fear amongst the women whocarried children on their backs and in their arms. The policeblew their whistles nervously and hit any black person that surrounded them.

Sarah feared for her son as she fought to push her wayup to the front to where Kungulu was. The more she tried tomove forward, the farther she was pushed back by the crowd.

"Gulu! Gulu!" She yelled over the people's screamsand shouts. Police sirens were heard from a distance andwithin minutes, they were at the scene. More white policeofficers filtered into the crowd with gas masks and nightsticks. Tear gas was tossed in the middle of the mob whichclouded the rioters' vision as the fumes burned the surface andstung the back of their eye balls. The officers clubbed theirway through the mesh of black people and the people whotried to fight them from being arrested were dragged away to be beaten, chained, and locked away in the police trucks. Oneofficer jabbed his night stick into a woman's stomach andcontinued to beat her as she helplessly fell to the ground andcurled up into a foetal position. He continued beating her andignored her shrieks and cries as she tried to protect her unbornchild.

A black man from the crowd saw the officer beatingthe pregnant woman and instinctively jumped the officer witha stone in his hand which he brought down on his head andrepeatedly smashed his skull to the ground until the officer layin a pool of his own blood.

"Gulu! Gulu!" Sarah was on the verge of tears, butshe was so frightened for her son that she could not cry. Thetear gas was the only thing that was blinding her and stingingher nostrils.

"Mama!" She heard his voice in the crowd and triedto follow it.

"Gulu!" She called out again. He answered her onceagain and for a brief moment, their hands met, but with therestless crowd between them, Gulu felt his mother's hand jerkaway from his. He yelled out to her nervously and with a loudcry, she yelled back his name. She was drifting from him. He tried to follow her voice which was fading to the outside circle of the crowd.

"Mama!" He screamed once more. His vision washazy, but he was able to make out a vision of his mother beingdragged off by an officer. He choked on the tear gas and triednot to lose sight of her. He saw the officer club her and punchher a few times before he threw her into the back of the policetruck which was made of blue iron caged doors. Gulu foundhis way to the truck just after the officer had locked the door.

"Mama" his voice cracked.She blindly called out to him and tried to push hertrembling fingers through the small squared barred windowand he reach out and gripped them. He looked up at her andhis foggy vision of a dark visage between the narrow bars.Her bloody fingers slipped from his grip and he fought tograsp them once again. She felt the blood rush down one sideof her face from a cut in her head. She was now blinded byher own blood and the stinging tear gas. The engine of the police truck started to rumble and Gulu's heart began to race.

Before he knew it, he was running after the truck in thecloudy dust it left behind. Gulu tripped over a rock and fell tothe ground and helplessly heard the truck disappear beforehim with his mother wailing out his name. He knelthelplessly and held his head in his hands.

Sarah sat in a flimsy wooden chair with her hands tiedbehind her back. Her head hung low while blood drippedfrom the tip of her nose from the gash on the side of her headwhere the police officer had clubbed her. One of theinterrogation officers pulled her head back by her hair andbrought his face close to hers.

"Now, tell me who was running the operation."

"I don't know. I was only there looking for my son.Please..."

"Shut up with your stupid lies. Who are you *really*? It will be for your own good to speak up."

"Sarah Zulu."

"Don't lie to me! You think we are stupid, eh?"

"No! No, I don't know what you want or what you are talking about."

"Okay, fine." He stepped behind her and untied herhands which were already bleeding from the friction of thetight rope. She opened her puffy eyes and all she could seewas a hazy figure before her and she could still feel the teargas stinging her eyes. She couldn't focus clearly, but shecould tell that there were three white officers in the room anda wooden table before her. The room had no windows and thedampness of the room filtered her nose and she could almosttaste the stale atmosphere. A single light bulb swayed above her head from a frail electrical wire which made the officer'sshadows move from east to west.

One of the officers with a thick moustache grabbed herhand and held it down on the table. With the other hand, heheld a night stick over her forefinger and grimly turned to herand said,

"Now, for every lie you tell, I smash one of your fingers with this." He waved his stick in her face and firmlygripped her wrist. "What is your name and who do you workfor?" He gritted his teeth and waited for her to answer.

"Sarah Zulu and I work for the Bellmonts in . . ." Before she knew it, the stick came smashing down on herforefinger and specs of blood splattered on the officer's face.

She let out a piercing scream and suddenly felt the room spin around her. She automatically lost consciousness and one ofthe other officers tried to slap her out of it. She could hearthem arguing, but she could not make out their faces anylonger.

"Now look what you have done. Why couldn't we just buzz her a few times with some electrical shocks? It'scleaner that way."

"How was I supposed to know she was going to faint again."

"Enough!" yelled the Commanding Officer. He wiped the blood off his face with his handkerchief and stuffed it back in his pocket. "Put her in a cell. Maybe shewill talk later."

Chapter Five

Kungulu woke up in a sweat and his chest felt tight as he tried to catch his breath. The nightmare was so real, so vivid, so threatening to his sanity. He could almost reach out and touch her with the tip of his fingers, and right before he could, he woke up perspiring. As usual, he was incoherent of his surroundings, and once he adjusted his vision, he didn't know whether to be relieved, or whether to be disappointed in the fact that he never finished the dream he was having. It was one of those dreams which left him dazed and confused about why things happen the way they do.

Today, as he had promised himself, was going to be a different day. He rolled out of bed, which was a mattress laid on the cold clay floor, and went outside to splash some cold water on his face. The cold bitter morning air numbed his nerves and the chill revived him back to life. He got on his bicycle and was on his way to deliver the morning paper. Although this was a daily routine for him, there was always something bound to happen on his paper route. Just the other day, he saw a black man get stopped by the police patrol and because he didn't have his identification papers on him, they slapped him around a couple of times and threw him in the back seat of their car. Only Lord knows if the man was released from their custody. The other day, a group of children going to school started to sing the freedom song at the top of their lungs when they saw two police officers driving around in their car. To mock the officers, they pulled their trousers down, shaking their bare back sides at them then they ran and disappeared down the road and alley.

Gulu always chose not to get involved. At times he even thanked God for his light complexion because the police didn't seem to bother him as much about his pass. On the other hand, other black men hated him and blamed him for the way he looked. This gave them a better reason to start getting physical with him.

As a child, he never really understood what it all meant, but now everything has fallen into place. He had learned to use the colour of his skin to his advantage. For one thing, it helped him get the job which pays much more than what most black men make. Not many black people could be trusted to deliver the morning paper from black townships to white suburban neighbourhoods. At this point, job opportunities have gone beyond racism. It is more about politics than anything else.

Politics, an essential route to understanding the laws of survival. The questions of why and how are only explained through the tertiary of politicians who make people act violently towards each other. Gulu lost his mother in a war she clearly tried to remain an innocent. In this world, innocent or guilty, you are always guilty if you are found in the wrong place at the wrong time. In the eyes of the black people, the white society has tried to do its best to keep their own lives as comfortable as possible. There was a point when the government encouraged tribalism as a way of making blacks fight amongst themselves. Unfortunately, it did not work. The blacks accepted their differences and learned to live and work together as one race to fight against the government.

The protesters are always students who are supported by their parents and teachers. The children have learned to carry a certain pride which has become clearer to them as teachers illegally taught them about Black American philosophy. They started dropping their school names - Mary, Peter, and Joseph - to African names like Tokologo which means freedom, Thokozile which means happiness, and Masechaba which means mother of the nation.

The words of great leaders and writers like Ted Tembo, Martin Luther King Jr., Desmond Tutu, and Nelson Mandela, rang in their ears. Every child knew and understood that Mtesa and Graceland will be one nation only if people learned to balance their character of good and bad and not seeing it as race relations, but as human relations. As Desmond Tutu said, "Africa may turn out to be not a Garden, but an anti-Garden, a garden ruled over by the serpent, where the wilderness takes root once again in men's hearts." Ted Tembo believed that if other black leaders could bring change to their nations, Gracelanders' tactics could also bring change to their country. "We should listen and not just hear words of freedom, it is only then that we can act upon our beliefs." At first, this seemed superficial to the people, but as they continued to ramp, rage, and believe in their struggle, the more they wanted freedom to come to them tomorrow.

Yes, freedom was coming tomorrow. Gulu believed in what Ted Tembo was saying. The black communities in the Shanty Towns and Townships were meeting privately to discuss their tactics in justifying their rights as citizens of Graceland. The only problem the government found with this was the immediate uprising of black power which could cause riots and confusion of the understanding of the status quo.

111

Because of the increasing violence in the streets between the police and the black people, the White Party banned the meetings the black politicians were having because they were said to "commemorate riots." They had press restrictions and had banned labour unions, youth associations, and the Immorality Act of sex across colours was strongly enforced.

With all these laws, freedom seemed to be a long way from home. Kungulu had been, and will always be, a strong believer in the utopian dream of unity. Everything will mysteriously work out in the end. Life seemed to work that way. One day, things will turn around and everyone will accept him for the way he was.

His thoughts trailed on through his mind as he parked his bicycle behind a brick wall where he hid it in the bushes. He climbed over the wall and into the back yard of the big white house. He quietly climbed the tree which led to her window where she was waiting for him. Before he could even crawl through the window, she kissed him passionately and he lost his fingers in her long blond curls.

Before noon, he was out her window and over the wall. He road on his bicycle down the hill and as the wind blew gently, he smelt her sweet perfume in his clothes and he automatically smiled to himself. He was now only a few miles from the Bellmont's house and it has now been a month since he passed by to see them.

Before he could even reach the front door, Mrs Bellmont came running out the door with her arms open wide. There was a time when she wouldn't even nurture him the way she was about to now. With a big wet kiss and a hug, she fussed with his clothing.

"Look at you, always looking a mess. Come on, uncle George is in the study. George, look who's here."

They entered his dim lit study and in a black leather chair behind a wooden desk, sat Mr Bellmont, sucking on his pipe.

"Well, look at what the cat dragged in. I was just thinking about you." He rose from his chair and shook Gulu's hand firmly. "Each time we see you, you are growing up into a nice young man."

"Yes, sir." Gulu smiled.

"What brings you to these parts?"

"George, he doesn't really have to have a reason to come and visit us, do you Gulu?"

"No, mum. I was in the neighbourhood and I thought I would pass by and say hello."

"How good of you, but we do wish you could come visit us more often. Ever since you and Catherine left home, the house has been very quiet. You do know that you can always come and stay with us for as long as you like." Mrs Bellmont spoke as tenderly as she always had. Gulu could tell that she was lonely. It has been five years since Catherine moved out and six years since Sarah died. Gulu has practically outgrown his teenage years and his voice wasn't cracking anymore. Now at the age of seventeen, he is living on his own in a shanty town with all the other black people who are trying to make it in the city world. Although he does not have much, he is still happy to have his health and memories of his mother, the few things which other people were unable to take away from him.

They sat in the living room and conversation took toll.

"What about Catherine?" Gulu asked. Mrs Bellmont sighed and with an air of disappointment in her voice, she began to explain.

"Her and her priest friend decided to elope and live out in the country where they could do God's work amongst the villagers. Munique left the church, but he says that he still practices his beliefs as a Christian. I always knew Catherine to be the odd ball out. Marrying a priest and making him give up his duties."

"Oh now, now dear. You know as well as I do that it wasn't like that. From what I remember, they were very much in love. God does work in mysterious ways you know." Mr Bellmont said as he patted her on the knee. It was strange for Gulu to see the two reverse their roles. There was a time when Mrs Bellmont longed for her daughter to find a husband because to her, it justified stability and security in the long run. As of now, Mr Bellmont seemed to be more concerned with his daughter's happiness. While they talked about their daughter, an invisible smile warmed Mr Bellmont's face. "It seems as though it was just yesterday that I taught her how to ride her first pony."

Gulu watched the old couple reminisce about their child. The way they talked about her seemed as though she was the only child they had. Charlie was never mentioned since the day Mr Bellmont kicked him out of the house. It was said that he had embezzled some money from Mr Bellmont's colleague's company. Then there were rumours going around about Charlie getting involved in illegal businesses like drug trafficking and smuggling jewels in and out of the country. Mr Bellmont stopped going to as many social functions as he used to because the shame grounded him. He now did most of hisoffice work at home while he hired certain individuals to run his other offices which were exposed to the public eye. Gulu thought about Charlie. What the hell was that evil man up to now?

The docks were darkened with the shadows of large crates and machinery. Each time the security night light rotated, it carried the shadows along the ground and onto the still water. Charlie waited coolly behind a crate with two other men. He glanced at his watch and looked around carefully. A few moments later, a Mercedes Benz pulled up in a deserted parking lot. A tall man in a long coat stepped out with a brief case in one hand. He made his way to the dock where Charlie and his companions were, and stopped about five feet in front of them. He put down his case and lit a cigarette. The light from his match quickly gave the others a glimpse of his sharp profile. Charlie stepped forward and only said four words.

"You got the money?"
The man nodded and blew smoke from the side of his mouth.

"Let me see the jewels." the man said. They both placed their treasures on a small crate and opened them. The briefcase was stacked with money, and Charlie's brown leather pouch sparkled with diamonds. The two men looked at each other and then they traded their riches.

"Where's the nigger?" The man asked.

"He's over there. Do you have the extra money for him?"

"Always." He gave Charlie a half smile and pulled out another wad of money from his breast pocket. To play it safe, Charlie had already had his hand gun at reach.

"Very good. I think we should do business more often." said Charlie.

"I never do business too often with the same people."

"As you wish."

They both went their separate ways with their exchanged treasures. Charlie left with the case of money and more, while the other man left with one of his black men and a leather pouch of diamonds. Once Charlie got in his car with his other colleague, he lit his cigarette before starting the engine.

"What is he going to do with the nigger?" asked his friend.

"That man, my friend, is a hunter. Instead of hunting red foxes, he hunts niggers for a sport." Charlie chuckled underneath his breath and drove away feeling satisfied with his mission.

Before the sun set over the African horizon and shadowed the trees of the suburban houses, Gulu left the Bellmont's estate so he could get home before curfew. As he approached the city, shop keepers were eagerly closing their stores while the last minute shoppers fumbled with their groceries and miscellaneous merchandises. A few more kilometres and he was almost home in Kompola.

Kompola is a humble little township where everyone lives in cramped conditions, and is an easy place to get lost in. There are no signs and every corner and house looks the same. The people from Kompola come from different tribes of Graceland. Like everyone else, Gulu has learned to pick up at least three different languages.

The only thing which the people of Kompola ever talk about is politics. If it wasn't politics theywere talking about, then it was sports. If it wasn'tsports they were talking about, then they weregossiping about their neighbours and who was havingan affair with whom. As much as Gulu liked talkingabout politics and politicians who he already knewabout like the back of his hand, he knew that hiscountry was drifting into an abyss of chaos. Even the names of things and places, like . . . Townships, is just an ironic compensating name for a poverty driven neighbourhood. All social gatherings in the eveningsalways ended with someone saying,

"Agh man, don't give me that rubbish. I am going to bed."

Their endless arguments about politics were monotonous. They almost made Gulu lose hope in Graceland in ever achieving an internal self-government. At this point, Graceland was far from even tasting the tip offreedom.

As he approached the outskirts of Kompola, he sensed the tension amongst the people. Something was going on which he did not know about. Nobody was talking and nobody was going to admit that there was anything wrong. Gulu looked up into the sky and instantly knew that tomorrow was going to be a very hot day. Earlier in the day, the moon had risen before the sun fell behind the earth, and now that it was dark, the moon was glowing red. Full and shaded with obstacles on its surface, the moon became the auburn sun of the night. An occasional dog started to bark and howl in the Township, but nobody dared to come outside their homes after curfew.

When Gulu was finally able to fall asleep, a gun shot went off and made him jump out of his bed. A woman screamed and voices of men yelled over her scream. Gulu looked out of his only boxed window and saw four silhouettes of which were two officers, a woman, and a man down on his knees. One officer had the man by the collar of his shirt, while the other held the woman back. Gulu went outside to get a better look at what was going on. It was his neighbours, Mangoliso and his wife Cecilia being raided by the police. Gulu knew that Mangoliso had occasionally had meetings at his house, but not many people knew about them.

"Please, please, don't hurt my husband!" Cecilia wailed. Gulu stepped in closer to see what was going on. One of the officers had grabbed Cecilia by the arm and was dragging her back into the house. The other police officer knocked Mangoliso on the side of his head with his hand gun and at that moment, Gulu's fist came flying into the officer's kidney. The officer fell and Gulu kicked him repeatedly in the head and in the stomach. He then helped Mangoliso to his feet and they both went into the house where they found Cecilia struggling with the other officer. Before he knew it, Gulu was punching the man in the face even after he had broken his nose. Mangoliso had to force him off the officer who now lay on the floor choking on his own blood.

"Go Gulu. Get out of he'e." Mangoliso said.

"No. I am not leaving until I know what is going on."

"It does not concern you . . ."

"Yes, it does. Now it does." He pointed to the officer on the floor who was now hanging onto his last breath. "Why were these men he'e? What did you do?" Mangoliso took a deep breath and ignored the wound on his temple. He felt it throb as blood kept flowing from his cut, into his ear and down his left shoulder.

"They found out about the secret meetings we've been having. Somebody from the inside let them know what was going on." He spoke in a softer voice as if he really did not want Gulu to know what he was going to say next. "We thought it was you, but after tonight,..." He couldn't even look at him in the face.

"What made you think I would tell anyone about something that I believe in?"

"Gulu you have to understand that it is because you are new around here and you also have to realize that in owa eyes, you are not completely black."

"I may look white to you, but I am as black as you are on the inside."

"Everyone is a suspect, Gulu."

"Don't give me that, man. I am fighting for the same thing you are! Agh man, what do you know?" He stormed out of their house feeling hated and disparagingly alone. He got on his bicycle and cycled down the street peddling like a mad man. He finally reached his destination at her house where he parked his bicycle behind the hedges. He climbed up to her bedroom window and tapped it gently until she woke up from a restless sleep.

"What are you doing here?" She whispered.

"Do you want to get yourself killed?"

"I didn't know where else to go." His eyes glistened with tears, but they were filled with love now.

"Come in before anyone sees you." They sat on the bed and she held his trembling hands. "You are shaking, what happened?"

"They blamed me for something I didn't do."

"What are you talking about?"

"Why is it that every time I try to stay out of trouble they always have a reason to point the finger at me?" She tried to find the answers in his face, but he had lost her. "Maria, do you trust me?" He asked.

"Of course I trust you. If I didn't, I wouldn't be with you." She placed her hand warmly on his face and held his gaze. He looked deep into her sky-blue eyes and lost himself in them. She kissed him gently on the lips and then lightly on his forehead, then his cheeks

119

and then on his lips again. Between kisses, he spoke softly into her mouth.

"Maria,... I love you." They continued kissing and he then asked, "Do you love me?" She did not answer. She continued kissing his lips and fingering his face with the tips of her fingers.

"Maria,"

"Shhhh. Don't talk." She whispered. Her warm kisses and soft touch put him in a trance. Once again, there was nothing in the universe but themselves.

Charlie became a natural born dealer. He dealt with smugglers, slave traders and black listed money hungry thieves. Charlie made more money than he had thought he would have made. Today was going to be a different day. He was going home to see his father. Once again, he was going to try and patch up things with the old man. He wanted his father to love him the way his friends loved him for his money, courage and great parties he always threw at his place. Although the young crowd loved Charlie, their parents loathed him and the kind of business he was in to. He was just praying that his father would not spit in his face the way that one woman did at the one dinner party he went to last week. Apparently, she blamed him for getting her son hooked on cocaine. Then he attentively told her, "Mrs Johnson, I am sorry your son is hospitalized, but he was the one who insisted on..." Before he knew it, his face was covered with her saliva. What a night that was. He spent half the night feigning that he was happy to be there. Erasing that thought out of his mind, he nervously attempted to tie his tie for the third time. He looked at himself in the mirror and then decided he didn't like the tie he was wearing.

"Geeze! I just might as well hang myself with this blooming' tie."

"Now, now, let me do it for you." A young and slender dark haired white woman crawled out of his bed and walked over to Charlie and started fixing his tie for him. "Take a deep breath and try to relax."

"No, you don't know my father Naomi. He is a bastard. Maybe that is where I get it from."

"Well if things don't work out this time, you can always try again. Whether he likes it or not, you are still his son. Blood is thicker than water, you know."

"Not in my family. If you don't live up to my parent's potentials, you are not part of the family." She finished tying his tie and neatly dusted the invisible dust off his shoulders.

"There. Now you look presentable." She kissed him gently, and then kissed him again, but this time, roughly like they had always played.

"Naomi," He pulled her away and slapped her with the back of his hand bringing her down to the floor. "I have no time to play! I just fixed my hair and you have to go off and put your filthy hands through it!" His hands were now shaking and once again he was nervous.

"I'm sorry," she spoke softly as she curled up in a foetal position.

"Don't you know how important this is to me, and you have to go off and..." He kicked her in the stomach and then said, "I will deal with you later! I have to go now." He walked towards the door and right before he walked out, he turned around and knelt down to where she was. He carefully raised her head up to his face and pushed her hair out of her eyes and gently wiped her tears. Tenderly and lovingly he uttered, "I am sorry. I am just a little nervous about this whole thing and..." His eyes swelled up with tears and he kissed her gently and then said, "I love you."

Like a wide eyed cat, she was still afraid to move an inch. She uncomfortably rested on one elbow and tried to smile. He smiled at her tenderly and then walked out the door.

The drive down to his parents' house was a quiet one. He had the radio turned off and the streets were empty. He had some time to clear his mind before he reached their front door. He looked at the front porch where he and his sister used to sit for hours talking until their mother called them in to go to bed. It was also the same front porch he had met Sarah and her mother for the first time. He had always loved Sarah, but he never knew how to show it. When he heard that she committed suicide in prison, he could not believe it. She was too strong of a woman to have wanted to take her life. Besides, she was living her life for that little coloured bastard she was raising.

He shook his head and cleared his mind of the past. He polished his shoes with the back of his trousers and touched his hair lightly making sure it was still in place. He took a deep breath, cleared his throat and rang the doorbell. Once he heard his mother's footsteps coming towards the door, his heart started racing. She opened the door, and much to her surprise it was her son.

"Hello, mother." He tried to smile and hoped that his mother would have some compassion in her face. Motionless, she stood there not knowing what to do.

"Dear, who is it?" His father's voice came from the back. When she didn't answer, he got up to see who it was. "Dear, who is at the..." He stepped in the door way and before him was his son standing nervously, hoping the tension would die over soon. He got in front of his wife and closed the door in his son's face.

Charlie stood there and waited. Not knowing what he was waiting for, he stood there for five minutes before tears started rolling down his face. He tried to move, but his feet were glued to the ground. He lowered his head and watched his tears drop and wet the tips of his shoes. Like a child, he wanted to be nurtured. He wanted to be held by mommy and daddy and to be told that everything was going to be all right.

When he was finally able to move his feet, he walked back to his car and sat in the driver's seat for a few minutes and cried at the steering wheel.

"Charlie," her soft voice startled him. When he looked up at his open window, it was his mother. She looked at him tenderly and put her hands through his hair. "He does love you, you know. He just doesn't know how to show it. She wiped his tears with her thumb and smiled at him.

"I love you mum." He kissed her hand that cupped his left cheek and savoured the moment before he drove off.

That night, Naomi got the beating of her life.

With his eyes fixated on a distant object outside the hospital window, Charlie knew that he had gone too far. He did love her. Really, he did. Please God don't let her die. She is all I have got. I don't know what I am going to do if she dies. In the middle of his internal prayers, a hand on his shoulder made him turn to face her father's anguished face.

"You have really done it this time. By God, you better pray that she pulls through because if she doesn't, you are going to pay for what you have done."

"Mr Jones, I love your daughter. . ."

"Don't patronize me. I know what you are all about and believe me; I will bring you down along with your filthy business. My God, I feel sorry for your parents. You are the devil's child, not theirs. They are good people, they are. Good people." On that last note, he walked away and Charlie turned back to stare at the object outside the window not thinking about anything. He found the urge to cry, but he couldn't. Something inside him bottled up the grief and he could not get it out. He wanted to cry. He wanted to let the pain out, but the fear kept him from letting go. He felt his heart sink down to his feet as he roughly put his hands through his hair, gripping it and wanting to tear every strand from the roots.

He took a deep breath to clear his head. Okay, I need to get myself together, he told himself. He needed to know where he went wrong. He needed to go back and fix the broken pieces and he knew exactly where he had to begin. His heart started to race as he walked down the empty hospital corridor. Soon enough, he found himself running down through the corridors and down the stairs to his car.

Gulu returned home and found his place ransacked. All his belongings were scattered all over the floor, his mattress was torn to shreds and his wooden table and chairs were broken to pieces.

"Gulu," Cecelia's silhouette was in his door way. "They came to look for you." Gulu knew who she was talking about. "You shouldn't have gotten involved because now they have put you on their black list." Her eyes filled with tears feeling frightened for him, she shuddered at the thought of what they may do to him. "They took my Mongoliso away." Her voice trembled as a lump formed in her throat. "You must go away from he'e."

He looked around his little home and pushed the broken furniture out of his way with his foot. He bent down to pick up the framed picture he used to have sitting on his bedside table. He brushed the grains of glass off the picture and sadly smiled at the picture of him and his mother standing on either side of Catherine. Catherine, the only person smiling in the picture, had one hand thrown over his mother's shoulders, and the other hand rested on top of his head. He was only six at the time. He took the picture out of the frame and carefully folded it twice and put it in his breast pocket. He then rummaged on the floor until he found the can of sugar he was looking for. He dumped the sugar on the floor and a small roll of money fell out from the bottom. He pocketed it and hugged Cecelia before he left. He had to go and find out what really happened and why it happened, and he knew where to go and who to go to find the answers.

Chapter Six

Gulu got off the bus smelling of chickens and goats. Even though the bus left him to choke on its dust, it felt good to get off the cramped vehicle. He was lucky to have not sat next to the man who was holding the little goat, which kept releasing droppings, which fell on the floor and were rolling between people's feet like little black berries. Gulu had sat next to a man who carried two plump chickens in a cage big enough for one. The eight hour bus ride was endless and exhausting. Before his stop, the bus only stopped once to let two people off and it wasn't enough time to get up and stretch. Even a little shut eye was impossible on the rough road. Every time he started to doze, the bus would run over rocks which felt like they had just run over some small wild animal.

Gulu threw his nap sack over his shoulder, took a deep breath and started heading for Polokoso. The sun beat down on him hard and by the time he reached the village, it was dressing the landscape with its sanguine rays as it set over the horizon. Two naked village boys saw him coming. They ran through the village yelling,

"Mbasa! Mbasa! Umukaladi aisa! Umu kaladi aisa!"

She stuck her head out of her mud hut to see what the noise was all about.

"Well, I'll be damned. Munique, look." Catherine ran out of the hut and threw her arms around Gulu. "Holy mother of God, it really is you."

Gulu's sun burned cheeks stung as she kissed them again and again. "Just yesterday, Charlie was here. I guess you both had lack of Catherine syndrome." She smiled.

"I never thought I would get here." Gulu sighed in relief and felt his chapped lips crack and sting.

"Come on. You are just in time for dinner." She linked her arm in his and led him to the inner part of the village where his lodging was, and then he was led to a clearing in the centre of the village where everyone congregated for a festive night.

That night, there was a celebration of dance and good food for a good season of harvest, and to welcome the new guest. As the food came out, they watched Gulu eat hungrily with his hands. Feeling embarrassed, he caught the eyes of two young girls with budding breasts giggling and shyly covering their mouths with their hands. He smiled back and tried not to feel like he was in a show case. On the other hand, it was nice to be admired by others for a change.

A fire was built in the middle of the clearing and the drummers pounded on their leather drums and the dancers came out to tell their story. The three male dancers synchronized their steps as they kicked their feet high above their heads forming whirl winds of dust around them. Their ankles and upper arms were skirted with dry grasses, their faces were hidden behind wooden masks and their chests scarred with significant lines of manhood. Followed behind them, was a young female dancer who was no more than Kungulu's age. She was the earthly toned beauty who had, and will continue to capture all the men's hearts in the village. Her neck was draped with hand polished beads, her waist wrapped in cloth, and her ankles tied with silver bells that jingled with every step that she took. Unlike the other dancers, her hair was braided back in corn rows to announce her African features, and her naked breasts and stomach burnished like brown velvet. Each step, each movement, each beat, and each voice told the powerful story of love, deceit, hunger and pain. Gulu could see it in her dance. Her movements were swift enough to catch up to the beat of the drums. She raised her hands and her head to the heavens and then to the earth, to the heavens, to the earth, to the heavens, to the earth. Her feet jingled and marked her trails. The male dancers danced around her, fought for her, marked their trails in the earth, and challenged each other for her. The dust rose, the drums roared and the voices soared until the dancers were lost in their own whirl winds of a phantasmagorical tale.

The whole time the performance was going on, Catherine watched Gulu. She tugged at Munique's arm so he could also see the awe in Kungulu's eyes.

"Look at him," she said. "He looks like he understands the whole thing."

"Why shouldn't he. It is in his blood."

Unshaven and clouded, Charlie arrived in his black jeep hoping he had gotten it right this time. On his way back from visiting Catherine, he got lost through the small forked roads in the country. He could feel and taste the dust between his teeth and the weight of his greasy hair, which had now grown passed his eye brows, needed to be tamed.

Once he arrived in his apartment, it was right before nine o'clock in the evening. Charlie lived like the ideal bachelor. Before he started to work, he grabbed a cold beer from his refrigerator and some left over baked beans and rice he had a few days ago. To give it more taste, he heated it up in a pan and sliced up a spicy sausage in it and added some salt, pepper and a little tomato sauce. It was at this point he started craving for a nice hot home cooked meal. Regardless, the meal was satisfactory and had hit the right spot.

He threw the dishes into the sink with the others and went into his little study. Unlike the other rooms of the apartment, his study was always in order. His files and paper work were neatly organized. Everything that he had done since the day he left home was in that office. He also had a confidential filing cabinet which had a combination lock on it which only he had access to. He sat down at his clean desk and put a sheet of paper in the type writer. He vigorously started typing a small brief of an illegitimate organization and before he knew it, it was dawn. He turned off his desk lamp and opened the curtains to let the sunlight in. He put the document in a neat pile at the corner of his desk and he went to take a quick shower. As he got dressed, he put on a dark blue pin striped suit. He looked himself over in the mirror and grabbed his briefcase with the document before walking out. He drove down to the first black prison on his list and parked outside the high electrical wired fence. Just to relax himself, he approached the guard coolly and chatted with him and even shared a cigarette with him before going in to see the Senior Chief Prison Guard. Once he got into the building, the officer outside his office said,

"You can't see him unless you have an appointment."

"Come on man, we are on the same side."

"Nowadays you can't tell. Do you at least have an ID?"

"Bloody hell, what for? Richard knows me. I am George Bellmont's son. In fact, he plays golf with my father." Charlie lied. It was something he had always been good at, especially in his profession. In the ten years he had not spoken to his father, he did not even know who his father associated with. For all he knew, the Chief and his father could be enemies. None the less, it worked. He found himself sitting in the office with the Chief, the man who should have been hunting down men like him. Instead he was killing innocent black people who always happened to be in the wrong place at the wrong time. Just like Sarah. She had been on his mind since he left Naomi in the hospital.

"What can I do for you?" bellowed the Chief Prison Guard.

"Actually, it is what I can do for you." Charlie handed him his brief and added, "I am currently trying to start a small organization to stop the chaos which our country is going through. We are a group of men who are trying to put a stop to the Union and Ted Tembo himself. They are causing too much havoc and confusion amongst our children and Tembo's beliefs are sabotaging the relationship our children once had with their parents."

"I do agree with you. What the Union is doing is really an ugly matter." He glanced at the brief and without looking up at Charlie, he said, "This is definitely a very important issue we should all be looking upon, but why have you come to me?"

Feeling relieved, Charlie could not believe how easy this was going to be. He crossed his legs and continued.

"Well, for starters, the majority of your prisoners are black activists and they are the key people we target. If you take a look on page nine, it explained to you how our psychologist has done some studies on how their preaching and lecturing has a tendency to build up a certain character in younger children. And this character results in "Black Power," which is the root of violence in our country. There are some key black people who have pushed this belief amongst the younger people to fight for equality, the main article which would probably mean taking jobs away from whites to blacks. "We have done a lot of research on this issue and we feel that if the blacks can have their own movement, so can we. I understand that you have a number of prisoners...specifically one by the name of..."

"Mr Bellemont, we don't carry names of prisoners in here. Once they enter the gates, they are given numbers. Each prisoner is associated with a number. Before we would call them one thing, they would want to be called another. It is the only way to keep these blackies in line." He chuckled. Charlie forced a smile on his face and added,

"I know what you mean." There was a brief pause in the conversation and then Charlie continued. "Apparently, the prisoners that I am looking for are women. I am looking to speak to a certain group of women who were arrested at certain period of time."

"I tell you what. Because I like what you are trying to do, I am going to help you out. I will let you speak to the whores as long as I or one of my men is there with you."

Charlie smiled again and they shook hands on that deal.

In order to get to the west wing of the prison, they had to walk through the north wing where the Chief explained was the detention centre of the children who assaulted officers in the process of refusing arrest.

Along with their echoing footsteps, Charlie could hear a resonant moan from one of the cells.

"Mama, Mama, Mama, Mama . . ." the soar voice continued. The further they walked, the closer the voice became. Soon, their footsteps met up with the voice from the cell it was coming from. The Chief got one of the guards to open the cell and the stench that came out of it, made Charlie queasy.

"What the hell is the matter with you?" yelled the Chief as he walked towards the young child who curled her bony body up in a foetal position in one of the dark corners. From what he could see, she was no more than ten. Then again, who could tell in the calamitous cell? The child continued to moan and the Chief finally signalled for one of the two guards that came with them to take care of her. He and Charlie continued on down to the west wing of the prison and at that moment, there were agonizing screams followed by thuds from the young girl's cell. Then they stopped. The slamming of the cell door and the clinking of keys were the last things they heard of that incident. Once the silence fell over, Charlie tried to mentally block it out, but his queasy stomach reminded him of the stench of that cell.

When he left the prison, before he could even get back into his car, he vomited. The guard who he had shared the cigarette with caught him before he fell over. Looking into his pale face, the guard asked, "Are you okay, man?" Charlie forced himself to focus and when he did, he forced himself up and stumbled into the driver's seat. "Are you sure you can drive? Let me get you some water."

"No! I am fine." Charlie insisted as he wiped his mouth with the back of his hand. He put the keys in the ignition and sped off down the road.

The more he tried to forget, the more he thought about Sarah. He had to find her. He got back to his apartment and cleaned himself up. He realized that he needed to get some more rest before going out again. Before the sun went down, Charlie was already in bed. He slept long and hard for the next twelve hours.

Gulu and Catherine sat on a large rock under a shady tree watching Munique try and fix the jeep.

"He is never going to get that thing fixed. He has been at it for months. I have seen more pieces come out of the jeep than I have seen him put pieces back." Catherine complained. She realized that Gulu was not listening to her. "All right, what's wrong? You certainly have something on your mind because the whole time you've been here, you have hardly said ten words."

"What makes you think there is something wrong?"

"Well, for one thing, you get these two wrinkles between your brows when something is bothering you. Just like your mother." she said.

"That's just it, my mother. In the few days I have been here, I now know what she meant by being proud of being not just being black, but being African. This place is probably like the village my mother grew up in, eh?" Catherine nodded. "She always used to tell me about her father, her brothers, my grandmother . . . When I saw those dancers, I saw my mother. She used to be a dancer, did you know that?"

"Yes, actually I did."

"She was beautiful wasn't she? She always told me that the people you love the most never die. While their bodies bring crop to the earth, their spirits live in memory and guide you and protect you. Cathy, you may think that I am crazy, but I don't think mama is dead. I keep having these dreams and, and....I don't know."

"Gulu, I don't think you are crazy. But I am sure there are a lot of things going through your mind right now. I can understand that you are scared and that you need your mother more than ever at this point in your life, but we all have to keep going."

"I can't. I don't think I can rest until I know what really happened to her. Even though the police told us that she committed suicide in prison, I don't believe one word of it. Mama was not the kind of person who would take her life. She would rather die from suffering than take her own life."

"Charlie said the same thing. I mean, about your mother being alive." She frowned to herself thinking about what he said.

"What?"

"Well, two days before you came, Charlie was here and he said the same thing."

"What would he know about my mother?" he said with disgust.

"Charlie loved your mother as much as you and I did. He just didn't know how to show it. Poor thing. His life is so messed up he can't seem to get out of it."

"Well, he drove himself to it. It's his own fault."

"Gulu," Catherine cut him off angrily.

"Sorry. But you have to admit that the feeling is mutual between me and him."

"Well, if you are not going to say anything nice about him, I would rather you did not talk about him at all."

"Fine." he shrugged his shoulders. Just like they had never changed the subject, Gulu picked up from where he left off. "Do you know that they don't even

135

keep records of all the people they arrest? Sometimes they arrest people and keep them locked up for so long they even forget why they locked them up for. When they arrested me, I was lucky. They asked me a few questions, gave me a bloody nose and then let me go. From that day on, I tried to keep a low profile and keep away from open demonstrations. It's hard, you know. Agh! But then you get so frustrated you find yourself getting involved again in underground uprisings and pray that you don't get caught. Before I came here, my home was ransacked and the police were looking for me."

"What did you do?"
"Two police men tried to kill my neighbour and tried to rape his wife, so I got involved. Now they are looking for me. I had to run away and stay out of sight for a few days. But even before that, mama was on my mind. It is more than just missing her. Something keeps telling me that she is alive."

"If you do find her, what then?"
"If she is dead, I will give her a decent burial. If she is alive, I will bring her back home."

Catherine put an arm around his shoulder and hoped that nothing would happen to him. She loved him like her own and did not want anything to happen to him. "Gulu, I don't want to lose you too. You know that I love you and that I would rather have you stay with me or mum and dad. But no matter what I say, you are still going to do what you want to do." She squeezed him close to her side and sighed helplessly.

Just at that moment, the engine of the jeep roared.

"My God, he actually got it started."
Catherine gaped in amazement and walked towards the jeep with Gulu.

"See, I told you I would get it running!" Munique yelled over the loud engine and stepped on the gas one more time to hear it roar again. With his face, hands, and clothes covered in grease, he jumped out of the jeep ready to throw his arms around Catherine, but she protested and stepped back.

"I love you Munique, but not with all that grease on you." Instead, he leaned forward and kissed her lightly. Gulu could see the love flow between them.

"One of us will have to take Gulu to the station, and it won't be you. You look like a spotted leopard." She commented.

"All right. As long as Manji comes along with you. I don't want you driving back alone. This jeep is still not in top shape." Once Gulu gathered his things, they were on their way with Manji, the tall dark Bantu, sitting in the back seat. Gulu strained his ears over the loud engine as he tried to listen to what Catherine was saying.

"I can't tell you what to do, but if you are going to ask questions in town, you have to ask the right people. I have a small black book in the glove compartment which has all the names and contacts of the few Black Activists who I used to help every now and then. It has been a while since I have been in contact with any of them. Some of them may be in exile, some in prison, . . . I don't know, but regardless, guard that book with your life."

"Cathy, why did you stop fighting?"

"I never did. Munique and I are still fighting, but only spiritually. There are two ways of fighting, Gulu. You could either fight by risking your life trying to kill the enemy, or you could fight by keeping the innocent people alive. Working out here in the village is a different kind of spiritual uprising. Munique and I teach them how to improve their crops and fight deceases.

137

Winning that kind of war is much more rewarding because you save more lives than you could ever imagine."

"You really love him, don't you? Munique that is."

"Yes. Even though it was hard for him to leave the church and for me to leave my clinic, it was worth it. It seemed as though you and Charlie were the only ones who were actually happy for us. I love Munique more than anything and I know that he is going to make a good father once this baby is born."

"You're pregnant? Sha! That's great!"

"Careful." She laughed when Gulu through his arms around her neck and made the car swerve a little.

Charlie walked through the third prison telling the warden the same story he had told the previous Chief Prison Wardens at other prisons. Down with Black Movements and up with White Supremacy. He couldn't believe how easy it was to make up radical patriotic jargon and get what he wanted.

Walking through this prison was not any different from the others. It was only now that the stale smell of urine and the gloomy cloudy walls were shadowed by a minor silence. Like the previous prisons, their footsteps echoed down the halls and around the corners. Before they started heading for the exit, a faint singing voice made Charlie stop dead in his tracks. It was so soft, so comforting,... and so familiar!

The warden turned to him and hoarsely said, "Yes, I know. Sometimes, even I stop to listen to her, but not too long. That voice is like a trance. These people can curse you with their ways, if you are not careful."

"Can I..." He listened some more. "Can I go and see her?" Before the warden could even answer him, Charlie had already started following the voice. It echoed throughout the west wing.

"You will never find her like that. Follow me." Charlie followed him and the closer they got, the more anxious he became. They got to the cell to where the singing was coming from. He looked through the little barred window in the rusted green door and only saw a shadow of a person crouched in one of the far corners.

"Can I go in?" He asked without taking his eyes from the figure in the corner. The warden clanked the keys in the key hole and creaked the rusted prison door open. The light filtered in and Charlie walked through it. When he knelt close to her, she stopped singing. She slowly turned to face him and blankly cocked her head to one side. With her left eye swollen shut, her sunken cheeks and lines on her face were, not only signs of aging, but were also signs of fatigue and suffering. He reached out for her bony hand and held it gently between his. The fingers were swollen and bent out of shape as if they were broken and had healed out of place. He caressed her rough hand tenderly, but she did not react. She turned her head back to where it had rested against the wall and started humming. Before he left, Charlie laid his hand on her head and felt the vibes of her humming go through him. He closed his eyes and swallowed hard, forcing the lump in his throat to go down. He could not believe that Sarah Zulu was alive.

That night, he lay in his bed awake. He had his hands clasped behind his head and was staring up at the ceiling. He thought about her and thought about her. Whatever happened, the image of Sarah Zulu was never going to go away. He closed his eyes and tried to force himself to sleep. When he did, his father came to him in a dream, like he had done before.

With black laced veils hanging over their faces, his mother and sister sat in church weeping before a varnished oak coffin with white lilies sprawled on top. His father's rhythmic footsteps knock on the marble floor as they approach the coffin and stood over and looked inside it with a vacant look on his face. Wide eyed, Charlie stared back up at him from the coffin and tried to call out to him to let him know that he was still alive, but no sound comes out of him. He tried to reach out his hand towards him, but he couldn't move. He strained his throat as he tries to call out to him again and again, but no voice comes out of him until he felt his lungs hurt. Still no voice came out of him.

His father just stared down into the coffin not seeing or hearing anything. He then muttered the unforgotten words,

"This is not my son."

Charlie quickly sat up in a pool of his own sweat feeling his heart pound vigorously like it was about to burst out of his chest. He looked around him breathlessly fighting the nightmare and when he finally caught his breath, he climbed out of bed feeling his knees shake as he walked to the bathroom. He splashed some cold water on his face before looking at himself in the mirror. He almost did not recognize himself. His tired and unshaven face had aged in a matter of days. The dark circles around his eyes and fringing strands of greasy hair were covering the residence of the young, handsome and youthful man his friends admired. Who was this man? Who was he turning into? What has he done with his life? Was it worth it anymore? He opened his medicine cabinet and pulled a razor out of a packet. He sat down on the bathroom floor and placed it against a blue vein on his wrist. His handswere shaking and his body shivered from a sudden chill that ran through him. He stared at his own strong hands and thought about Sarah Zulu and her hands. Those hands were once beautiful hands. She did not choose to be in prison, yet she was being punished for someone else's crimes. His crimes. Now that he found her, how was he going to get her out of there? Finding her was the easy part. Getting her out seemed to be a mission impossible. He couldn't think anymore. Everything seemed to come to a dead lock.

He threw the razor to the floor, gripped his curtaining hair and began to cry.

"How did you know where to find me?"

"Catherine Bellmont, she used to be an old friend of yours? Well, she told me that if I ever needed any help in finding someone, to come to you." The man studied Gulu through the small crack he had made through the door. Still frowning, he looked Gulu up and down, and right before Gulu thought he was going to shut the door in his face, the old man opened the door a little further and said,

"Come in."

Gulu walked into the small dark living room. The bedizen cloth on the furniture was faded with age, and the faded holey blue curtains which were made out of bed sheets kept the bright afternoon sun out. Gulu carefully sat in one of the chairs feeling the springs and the wood creak under him. The old man sat across from him still frowning with curiosity."What do you want from me, child?" He asked suspiciously.

Gulu began to tell his story about how his mother was arrested and how he believed that she was still alive. When he was finished, the old man leaned back in his chair and stared at him and pondered upon what the young boy was saying.

"I can't help you." he finally said.

"I don't understand. Why? You are my last hope and she is the only family I have."

"What about your father?"

Gulu shrugged his shoulders and replied, "What about him? I don't even know who he is or where he is. Neither does my mother, nor does she wish to know."

"Listen child, I am an old man. I haven't worked with the Union in years, the government has black listed me, and if they know that I have su'faced again, my wife will kill me. I have my family to think about."

"So do I. Look, all I am asking is for you to just help me. I am not asking you to become active again."

"No, I can't." He responded sharply. He looked away from the boy remembering how they had tortured him during his interrogation seven years ago. He could still feel the stinging electric shocks go through his body and boil his blood every time he did not say what they wanted him to say.

"They arrested you and tortured you and tried to brain wash you too, didn't they?" Gulu had read his mind. The old man tensed up inside and tightly gripped his chair with his fingers.

He did not look at Gulu. He kept staring at one of the holes in the curtain where a thin ray of light was coming through.

"I think you should go now."

"Please . . ."

"No!" He darted his eyes at Gulu and did not blink. "You think you can come he'e and demand me to

142

help you find a whore who you call your mother, well you a'e wrong. I have suffad enough and now I am old, tiyad and the last thing I need right now is you coming he'e asking for favas when I can barely take ca'e of my family. Go back to whe'e you came from. Go you, go I say! Little coloured basta'd. You don't know what it's like to be me! You just don't know!" He turned away from him so he wouldn't see the tears in his eyes. He didn't say anything and waited until Gulu let himself out of the house.

Gulu felt so torn up inside he didn't even know what to do next. He flipped through the little book and blankly looked at the names. He couldn't go through that again. What if they all turn him away like the old man did?

It was starting to get dark and he needed a place to sleep. He couldn't go back to his old house and he couldn't go to his girlfriend's house at this time. It was too risky. That night, he crouched in an alley of an old building and fell asleep using his nap sack as a pillow.

Before he knew it, the city was alive again. He squinted his eyes towards the main street and thought about what to do next, but first thing was first. He had to get some food in his stomach. He walked along the street where he knew there was a little restaurant where they served a good breakfast. He knew the owner from his newspaper route. The man would occasionally give him a hot cross bun straight from the oven.

"Ah Gulu, whe'e you been? I was expecting you the other day until I saw another boy delivering your papers."

"Well, I got myself in a little bit of a mess. The police are after me."

"You? A good boy like you? What you do?"

"They started beating up my neighbour and so I went to help him."

"Always trying to do right, you are. Come; let me make you something to eat. If they come he'e looking fo' you, I never saw you in my life." The jolly full faced light skinned black man let out a hardy laugh and patted Gulu on the back.

Gulu ate hungrily like he had never eaten before.

When Johnny opened the door to Charlie's apartment with his spare key, he did not expect to see his childhood friend passed out drunk on the floor at the foot of his bed with a half empty bottle of Johnny Walker's Whisky in his hand. Yes, Charlie had been drunk and high before, but this was different. He looked like hell. He knew that things were bad between him and Naomi, but not this bad. He helped him into the shower and let cold water run down on him hard until he started coming around. After an hour of rejuvenating him along with a hot cup of coffee, Charlie was coherent of what was happening.

"How long have you been like this, man?"

"I don't know, two days, maybe."

"When you didn't show up yesta'day at the stables to meet owa new deala, I got worried. It was supposed to be one of owa biggest shipments in months and I knew how much you were counting on this deal of diamonds. You never miss a good deal."

"Johnny, that deal is the least part of my problems." He took a sip from his mug and felt the hot coffee burn his throat and warm up the walls of his empty stomach. "Naomi is in hospital because of me and her father won't even let me see her, my father still hates me, . . . but I've still got my health, right?" He added sarcastically.

"Oh, Charlie,"

"Yeah, I really hurt her bad this time. I almost killed her, you know. I don't know what came over me, but I was so angry at myself that I took it out on her."

There was a comforting silence between them while Charlie took another gulp of his coffee. Without looking at him, Charlie asked,

"Johnny, have you ever seen the inside of a black prison before?"

"No, what for?"

"I have. Just the other day."

"What the hell were you doing there, and how the hell did you get into one?" Charlie's knuckles turned white as he gripped his coffee mug tighter. He impetuously stared into it and watched the steam rise to his face.

"I saw her Johnny, I saw her there."

"Who?"

"She doesn't deserve to be there and I put her there." He fought the tears that came back again, but this time, they only blurred his vision.

"Naomi?"

"After so many years, I never thought she could look so different. But you know what? She still sings like an angel."

Johnny sat and listened to his friend talk in phrases he did not understand. Either Charlie was going mad or he needed to lay off the liquor and grass he was smoking. He wasn't making sense anymore. He looked at him hard and tried to see if he could figure him out, but nothing seemed to come clear to him.

"I loved her and I let this happened to her, Johnny."

"Charlie, I want you to get dressed because we are going to go out for a walk so you could clear your head, okay?"

"Okay." he obeyed.

Charlie was moving in slow motion while Johnny helped him get dressed in a clean shirt and pair of jeans. Once they got outside, Charlie felt the sun sting his eyes and the warmth of it actually made him feel better. They stopped at a little food stand and Johnny bought two large sandwiches for the both of them. He encouraged Charlie to eat because he needed to get his strength back. They sat on a bench in a park sectioned off for whites and watched the people go by.

"How do you feel?" Johnny asked him.

"Good. Thanks."

Johnny took a deep breath and sighed.

"For a minute there, you scared me. I thought my best friend had gone mad when all you needed was some food in your stomach. Next time you feel hungry, just let me know, okay? You are living proof that hunger can cause madness, eh?" He opened up a pack of cigarettes and offered one to Charlie.

Gulu walked toward the park wondering what to do next. There had to be someone who could help him out. He took out the little black book and glanced at the names until his eyes fell upon the name Susan Kapepe. It sounded familiar, but he couldn't quite place it. Without looking where he was going, he bumped into a gentleman in a white suit and hat, and dropped his book.

"Watch it!" He growled at Gulu. Gulu quickly picked up his book and apologized, but not loud enough for the gentleman to hear him. The gentleman frowned at him and grumbled, "Idiot." He saw that the coloured boy kept walking so he called out to him. "Hey, boy! I am talking to you." Gulu kept walking.

"I said I am talking to you." He grabbed Gulu by his shirt to turn him around, and said, "What the hell are you doing walking on this side of the park? Can't you read? The sign over there says, 'Whites Only.'"

"Yes, actually I can." He said confidently. "It seems as though you are the one who needs to get your eyes checked because I am white." Caught by surprise, the gentleman's back hand came flying across Gulu's face.

"You couldn't be white even if you tried, nigger." Right when he turned his back on Gulu, Gulu jumped him from behind and pulled him to the ground. When the gentleman finally had him pinned down to the ground and was ready to thrash him with his fist, he was pulled up from behind by the collar and before he knew it, he was on the ground with his hands cupping his bleeding nose. The stranger then turned to Gulu and grabbed him by the arm. Gulu began to struggle from his grip until the stranger
said,

"Hey! It's okay, it's only me!"
Gulu stopped struggling and found himself face to face with Charlie. Caught by surprise, he still jerked his arm away as he stepped back. The gentleman was still struggling to get up on his feet with one hand cupping his nose. In his muffled voice, he turned to Charlie and said,

"What the hell do you think you are doing? I should have you both arrested."

"We should have you arrested for assaulting a minor. Now get the hell out of here before I make you eat your hat." Charlie said as he gritted his teeth. The gentleman staggered off holding his nose and his hat in the other hand. "Are you alright?" He asked Gulu. Gulu didn't answer. Speechless and wide eyed, they both stared at each other for a moment feeling paralyzed. Gulu was staring into the eyes of the man who once antagonized him ever since he could remember, and Charlie was staring into the eyes of a boy who he remembers being apprehensive around him. Finally, Gulu made the first move by picking up his things and starting on his way. "Wait," Charlie stopped him. Gulu turned around and didn't say a word. "Where are you going?" Without answering, Gulu turned back around and started on his way again. Charlie then yelled out, "409 Parker Street..... If you need anything...that's where I stay." Johnny approached Charlie feeling angry and baffled about the whole incident. Seeing him jump to his feet and run to save a coloured boy was something Charlie never would have thought about doing in a million years. He would have sat back, watched, and then laughed about the whole incident. Something had happened to him, and Johnny didn't like it.

"What the hell has gotten into you?" He started with him in his thick Gracelander accent.

"If I told you, you would think that I was crazy."

"Well, too late. I already think you're crazy, man. Bolloxing your girl, talking about black prisons and now protecting a coloured?!? Yes, you really have lost your mind if you ask me!"

"If I tried to explain it to you, you wouldn't understand!"

"If you would talk to me and tell me what is going on, maybe I could try to understand what is going through your head!" Before he could say anymore,

Charlie walked away in long strides towards his apartment. Johnny followed behind him cursing underneath his breath.

They both walked into his apartment without speaking to each other. Charlie went to the refrigerator and pulled out a cold beer for himself, and Johnny stood in the living room watching him guzzle the beer down.

"Come on man, you don't need to. . ."

"Don't tell me what I need right now Johnny!" He slammed the bottle on the table making it foam to the top. "Nobody knows what I need. I don't need you telling me what is good for me, I didn't need Naomi who was just a silly cow in my life, and I certainly don't need you coming here to judge me and criticize me for everything that I do! If you really must know, yes, I am in love with a black woman. Yes, I dream about being with her and making love to her, and yes, I am giving up my bigot life for her. Is that what you want to here?"

"You are mad."

"Yes, me the insane, the coo coo, and the crazy man...whatever the hell you want to call me. I am the same man who can out smart any con artist and out run any law officer. I am the one who taught you the tricks of my trade. I made you into the rich bastard that you are today, Johnny! If it wasn't for me, you would be shovelling dung for a living!" He took another swivel from the bottle before he smashed it against the wall.

Johnny was disgusted with Charlie. "Making love to a black woman? Giving up his life for her? What the hell has gotten into you?" Jonny yelled back. The room grew silent and the last thing that was heard was the closing of the front door when Johnny left the apartment.

149

Samra, middle classed neighbourhood populated by blacks, was quiet. The only people, who were out and about, were three girls playing jump rope, an old man trimming his hedges, and a grandmother rocking in her rocking chair on her porch pretending to be reading when she was actually watching Gulu.

He knocked on the wooden door of a white picturesque house at the corner of Bishop Street, but nobody answered. He knocked again and tried to peep through a crack between the closed curtains of the living room. Everything seemed to be still in the house. Feeling disappointed, he started to walk out of the yard through the small front gate when the old woman said to him in her strong black Gracelander accent,

"Theya nobody home. What you want with Miss Susan, child?

"Do you know where she's gone to?" he asked.

"She at wo'k. Sometime when she wo'k late, she don't come back at all because of curfew."

"Thank you." He said, and started on his way. It was almost curfew and he was never going to make it back into town in time. He felt for his papers in his pocket to make sure they were still there. He then made sure that his little black book was safely tucked away into his sock before he started jogging back into town.

Charlie sat on the couch watching TV. Between his fingers, he held a cigarette with half of its long smoking ashes still lingering on the end of it. He wasn't drinking though. The TV flickered before him as he pensively thought about what he was going to say to Gulu once he saw him again. He had always hated the little bastard, but for once in his life, he felt that it was important for him to do something for Sarah Zulu. It was the least thing he could do. Although it has been years since he last saw Kungulu, he had recognized him on the spot in the park.

He remembered him as a child who always walked around with his nose in a book, magazine or newspaper, just like he was doing in the park. He never really had any friends, but for a brief moment there was one little coloured girl he used to play with, but she stopped coming around. Another thing which Charlie remembered about him was that there was always an angry streak in him. He always used to get into fights at school. Charlie knew this because he would see and hear Sarah scolding him time and time again for fighting. Because of his fighting, he could never stay in one school for more than six months. Or was it a semester? Anyway, for a kid like that, it was hard to believe that this was the same kid who was so quiet around the house that nobody really knew he was even there. Weird. Very weird. Despite that fact, everybody liked him. Catherine, his mother, his father, the gardener.....everyone. There was a quick and subtle knock at the door. Charlie turned down the TV and listened again. There was nothing. Just to make sure that he was not hearing things, he got up to open the door. There he was, standing before him, was Gulu with his traveling bag thrown over his right shoulder. The young vagabond could barely hold Charlie's gaze and their silence made him feel uneasy. Gulu thought about turning around and going back into the streets, but the two policemen who were standing under a street light at the corner, were going to be hard to get around, and the last thing he needed was to be thrown in jail for being outside during curfew.

"I.....It .....it is after curfew and I didn't know where else to go." He said nervously. They stared at each other for a moment before Charlie realized the boy was still standing outside the door.

"Sorry, Come in." Charlie finally said. Gulu came in and stood in the middle of the living room looking around him. "Please, sit down." Said Charlie, and he quickly started picking up clothes and old newspapers off the floor and chairs. Gulu uneasily sat on the couch and started wondering what he was doing there. Charlie crumpled up the last newspaper and tossed it in his office and closed the door.

"Can I get you anything? Something to drink? Something to eat maybe?" Gulu shook his head.

"I am just really tired, that's all." He answered.

"Oh, okay. I'll just get you some bedding then. This apartment may look big, but I only have one bed. If you don't mind taking the couch..."

"That's fine, thank you."
Charlie came back with a clean blanket and a pillow and said,

"The bathroom is right over there and if you get hungry, there is some,...well, actually, I don't think I have much in the kitchen, I haven't done any grocery shopping in a while... well anyway, help yourself to anything and if you do need anything, I will be in my room. Are you sure you don't need anything? I could always make you something."

"I am fine. Thank you. I just need some sleep, that's all."

"Okay," He stood around for a few seconds until he realized that Gulu wanted to be alone. He then said good night and went off into his room. He lit another cigarette and filled his lungs with smoke and realized how stupid he sounded. He fell back on his bed and watched the smoke linger above his head and thought, oh well, there is always tomorrow.

When dawn broke, the orange rays carpeted the roofs of the neighbourhood houses. As Charlie slept on his back, a bright ray shone through his open window and onto his eyes forcing him to slowly wake from his sleep. Still half asleep, he dragged himself to the bathroom, and when he was done relieving himself, he went to check on Kungulu. He was gone.

He quickly looked out of his window and saw him walking down the street with his bag thrown over his shoulder. Charlie pulled on the pair of jeans that he had worn the day before and rushed downstairs without putting a shirt or any shoes on. He followed Kungulu closely, but discretely. He watched him walk two blocks down, around the corner and three houses down, is where he stopped to climbed a tree to the bedroom window of a big white house. He saw a young blond girl open the window and embrace him and let him into her bedroom. Charlie smiled to himself and shook his head.

"Well, what do you know..." he said to himself. He sat on a rock and waited. Forty-five minutes later, Gulu was climbing out of the bedroom window and was on his way.

"You know you can get yourself into a lot of trouble for sleeping with Mr Steven's daughter. Everybody in this neighbourhood knows that he is no nigger lover."

Gulu was surprised to see Charlie come out from behind the bushes by the house standing there and slyly smiling and almost laughing the words at him. He decided to ignore him and keep on walking. "Girls like that don't really care about boys like you. They only do it because they are curious about coloured boys and black boys. It's only a phase she is going through, you know."

"You don't know anything about her or me."

"I don't need to. I know her type. Her father thinks she is the innocent virgin who doesn't do any more than sing in a church choir, but little does he know, she runs around with every man or boy that she can get her hands on. My friend Johnny will tell you. He had her once and he can tell you that she does more than sing in a church choir." He snickered. Gulu became angry now. He jumps at Charlie and threw a wild punch and missed Charlie as he ducked. Charlie quickly manoeuvres him into an arm lock so tight that Gulu thought he was going to break his arm.

"Let me go!" Gulu gritted his teeth.

"Not until you promise to come back to the apartment with me."

"Why? What do you want from me?"

"I just want to talk, that's all. Now, I am going to let you go and I want you to promise not to run away, okay?"

Gulu hesitated and then answered,

"Okay."

As soon as Charlie unlocked him, Gulu sprinted down the street and Charlie ran after him in his bare feet. They ran through the neighbourhoodand around the corners and back into town wheretraffic on the sidewalks and on the streets wasbuilding up to a busy morning. What they didn'tknow, was that ahead of them was a group of policeofficers questioning two black men about theirpapers. One police officer saw Gulu knock down apedestrian, and before he could even make his waypassed the officers, one of them quickly grabbed himright before he ran past.

"And where do you think you are going, eh?"He said to Gulu and held him up by the collar of his shirt. Gulu tried to shake the officer off until the officer put his gun to Gulu's head and threatened to shoot his brains out if he tried to get away.

"Come on, man. The boy didn't do anything."Said one of the two black men who were being interrogated. The people walking by stopped to watch the commotion.

"Shut up! Who asked you?" yelled the officer. At that moment, Charlie came around thecorner and saw what was happening. He stopped tocatch his breath and started to walk towards them.

Just at that moment, the other people who were watching got involved. Within a matter of seconds, a fight broke out. The blacks against the white police men. The police men who were outnumbered were on the ground and were being kicked by the blacks. Gulu was caught in the middle of the squabble and Charlie tried to push his way through to get to him. In the process, he got kicked in the head and in the ribs. When he finally got to Gulu, he grabbed him out of the mob and they both staggered to the other side of the street. After the kick in the head, Charlie started feeling dizzy and faint. He tried to sit down on the curb, but Gulu tugged at his arm to make him move.

"Get up! We have to get out of here before the other police get here." Charlie held Gulu's hand and staggered behind him. He had no choice, but let Gulu be his guide to safety. Once they were clear from the mob, he stopped to let Charlie sit down a while. He saw the blood trickle from a small cut on Charlie's temple. "Are you all right?" He asked.

"As soon as I stop seeing two of you I will be fine. Where the hell are we?"

"Carefree Avenue. Your place isn't too far from here."

"Geeze," Charlie said to himself as he felt his head throb. "If you would have listened to me, this wouldn't have happened."

"If you wouldn't have followed me, this wouldn't have happened. Now go home and leave me alone."

"How the hell am I supposed to get home if I don't know where the hell I am?"

"As long as you don't go past Minister Street, you will be fine. The blacks there wouldn't hesitate to skin you alive." Said Gulu, and he started walking away.

"Thanks. That really helps," he said sarcastically. "…but I don't think you are going to get very far without your address book." Gulu quickly rummaged through his bag and found nothing. "It is amazing of what a light sleeper you are. I pulled it right out of the smelly sock you were wearing and tucked it away in a nice safe place. Now if you get me home and don't try to run away, that book will not end up in the wrong hands."

"It already has." Gulu said. "Follow me."

Chapter Seven

Okay, I brought you to your place; now give me back my book."

"Not until you sit down. I want to talk to you.""Agh man, what is there to talk about? You hate me, I hate you,... I guess we have a lot in common, eh?"

Charlie's head throbbed from all angles. The blows he got to the head made it hard for him to think. He tried to keep himself calm as he attempted to explain himself. He took a deep breath and frowned,

"Look, I know that if I told you, you wouldn't believe me, so the best thing for me to do is show you."

"Show me what? What the hell are you talking about?"

"Let me just get dressed and cleaned up and then we are going for a drive. Trust me."

"You expect me to trust you? A Muzungu? You must be out of your mind."

"You know what? I have been hearing too much of that lately. I am not out of my mind and even if I was, why the hell would I save your coloured behind twice in two days? All I am trying to do is do you a favour."

"I don't need favours from you, honky."

"Now, there is no reason for you to be calling me names."

"I have every reason to."

"Then why the hell did you come to me when you didn't have anywhere else to go?"

Gulu didn't answer and his face remained tight and subdued. Charlie was frustrated, angry and his patience for Kungulu was running out. He felt a dizzy spell come on when his vision blurred and he almost lost his balance. Before he fell over, he sat down on the couch and rubbed his temples. Gulu was a little worried, but he didn't want to show it. With his eyes still closed, Charlie began to talk calmly.

"Look, you can call me what you want, honky, crazyman, a Klan man, whatever. No matter what happens, you need me. There is no other way to tell you this, so I might as well tell you." He took another deep breath, rested his head back and fought the pain in his head. "I saw your mother the other day and believe it or not, she is alive."

Gulu didn't say anything for a moment. Charlie opened his eyes to make sure that he wasthere. Sure enough, Gulu was looking at him stifflyand uncertain. "I saw her, Kungulu." Gulu still didn't say anything. He was still paralysed by thenews.

"You are lying." The bitter words came out of Gulu. "It's true. I saw her." Charlie leaned forward in his chair and looked Gulu straight in the eyes to prove to him that he was not lying. "I would never lie about something like this. If I am lying then let God strike me down right now, right here. Kungulu, your mother is alive and she wants to see you."

Gulu still did not blink, breathe or even find the voice that once came out of him unexpectedly. He had finally heard the words he had longed to hear. His mother was alive. He was hearing Charlie speak and he watched as the words came out of his mouth, but he wasn't listening anymore. But why should he believe Charlie? This was the same man who hated him from the first day they met, and all of a sudden he wanted to help him? Why?

"She doesn't look very well and if you want to see her, you will have to do exactly as I say. Do you understand?" Charlie explained to him. Gulu wasn't studying his face anymore. He just vacantly looked at him. "Do you understand?" Charlie repeated. Gulu eased himself down on the couch and stared at the floor. "Just give me a chance. Trust me." Gulu said nothing. He was still oblivious. Charlie knew that this was the right time to go get cleaned up while the truth sunk into Kungulu's head. Charlie changed out of his bloody clothes; he cleaned and dressed the cut on his temple. Obediently, Gulu got in the car with Charlie and blindly stared out the windscreen. When Gulu finally realised where they were going, he turned to Charlie and asked,

"What the hell are we doing here?" Charlie carefully read the signs on each corner and nervously drove through the black neighbourhood.

"We're here to see a lawyer, Susan Kapepe. We will need her help to get to your mother. She was in your little black book. I recognised her name, but I couldn't remember where I had heard that name. After a few phone calls, it finally came to me. She is the first and only practising black woman lawyer in Graceland. I spent half the night making phone calls and reading about her and the kinds of cases she has done. She is the best there is from what they say. She lives somewhere around here." He carefully looked at all the numbers on all the houses as he drove by them slowly.

Gulu looked at him and thought about the kind of man that Charlie really was and how everything he did, he did for a reason.

"Why are you doing this?" He finally asked him.

"I am not doing this for you, if that's what you're thinking. I am doing this for your mother. Someone like her deserves better. I know that I was not her favourite person, but I would never wish the worst upon her. After I heard that she was dead, I couldn't believe it. I didn't want to believe it. It wasn't like your mother to take her own life. I guess my instincts were right. She is a good person and I feel responsible for what happened to her."

Gulu thought to himself, that what Charlie was saying, was not making any sense. He was not telling him the whole truth. But at this point, he knew that Charlie needed him as much as he needed Charlie. Without looking at Charlie Gulu gave him the directions.

"She lives on the corner of Bishop Street. Turn left at the intersection and it is the house on the left." Charlie parked the car outside the house and they both walked up to the front door. Gulu saw that the old lady from across the street was watching them. She was sitting in same rocking chair and was reading the same book she was reading the previous day. It was as if she had not moved from the previous day. Charlie knocked on the door twice before a tall attractive woman in a beige bathrobe opened the door. Revealing her flawless skin and graciously long neck, she had her hair tightly pulled back in a bun.

"Yes, may I help you?" She said in her cunning voice and glanced at the two strangers on her door step.

Charlie cleared his throat and started to do all the talking. He introduced himself and for the first time in his life, he was going to tell the truth. Susan Kapepe half listened and half studied the young coloured boy who was with him.

"Would you like to come in?" She interrupted Charlie.

They walked into her house and they were both taken by her simple, but posh décor. The marble floor and the large living room carpeted by a Persian carpet that stretched across the room towards the dining room. Two pastel paintings, one of impalas running through the safari, and another of a lioness bathing her two cubs, hung in the living room over her cream coloured couches. Two wooden carvings of giraffes stood tall on either side of the front door. "Please, sit down." She said. Charlie and Gulu glanced at each other before they sat across from each other on the soft cushioning couches. "Some tea?" She offered.

"Yes, please." Answered Charlie. Gulu smiled and nodded politely. When she returned, she placed the tray in the middle of the glass table and served them their tea.

"I have heard so much about you." Charlie continued from where he left off. As he talked, her eyes kept trailing into Gulu's direction. She finally sat back and folded her arms and pensively looked at him.

"Kungulu." She said allowed, interrupting Charlie. Puzzled, Charlie stopped and wondered whether he had missed something. "I remember you," She pointed her forefinger at Gulu and squinted one eye. "You were little Camellia's friend. She always talked about you." She kindly smiled and began to explain to Charlie who was a little lost in the conversation. "Five years ago I defended a little girl about Kungulu's age." Remembering she smiled to herself. "I remember she was such a beautiful child. Unfortunately, I lost the trial and there wasn't much I could do for her." Her expression changed as she remembered the bitter part of the memory. "I never forget the trials I lose. Always learn from your mistakes, I tell myself." She remembered her guests and she smiled at Gulu warmly. "How is she? I tried to keep track of her whereabouts, but with the kind of father she had, he made sure nobody got into his family affairs after that trial."

Gulu frowned at the woman and his hands got clammy as he nervously rubbed them together. He was remembering. He was remembering the things he forced himself to forget many years ago. He remembered the weeping willow by the lake and Camellia trying to wash away the blood from between her legs. There was so much blood. So much blood that it kept flowing and she kept crying. He couldn't stop the bleeding. She was crying and was in pain and he couldn't help her. Gulu worked up a sweat as the memory came back stronger and stronger. He had to get out of there. He jumped out of his seat and dashed out of the house without closing the door behind him. Charlie went after him down the street and Susan followed on after them.

"Where the hell are you going?" Charlie called after him.

"Away from here. I don't want to have anything to do with that woman or any of this anymore."

"What do you mean? Was it because that woman knew you? Or is it that Camellia girl?" Abruptly, Gulu spun around and darted his eyes at him.

"Don't you ever mention her name to me again! You knew nothing about her nor do you know anything about me! Who the hell do you think you are, bringing me here? Who the hell is this woman anyway? Is she part of your big plan? For once in your life, why don't you tell me what you want? What do you really want from me? What do you want from my mother? Who the hell are you, anyway? I can see right through you, Charlie. You say that you are doing this for her, but you have never done anything for anybody, but yourself!"

Charlie raised his back hand, but he stopped himself before he let it come down on Gulu's face. The words finally exploded out of his mouth like a tidal wave.

"I loved your mother! Yes, I was stupid enough to not have told her years ago, but I am making up for it now. Maybe you are right. I am being selfish because I want your mother to myself. In fact, I have always wanted her to myself."

"What do you mean you want her to yourself? You never had her."

"Yes, but she had me. She had me tied up in knots thinking about her day and night! She had me going crazy each day I didn't see her, she ..."

"Why don't you just leave us alone? She is all I have and you want to take her away from me! You have your family, your money and your white world. What more do you want?"

"I don't have anything! Nothing is worth more than the love your mother and I shared. She was my world, she was my life." Charlie swallowed hard and could not beat the salty tears that filled his eyes. "I don't have anything if I don't have what money can't buy." Painfully, Gulu also started to cry.

"So, you want the only thing I have. I am a bastard and I have been called a coloured bastard all my life. There have only been two people in this world, my mother and Camellia, who never looked at me that way." He swallowed hard and pulled away when Charlie tried to reach for his shoulder. The old lady from across the street had been watching the two strangers quarrel and she had put her book down to watch what was going to happen next.

Gulu rubbed his eyes with the sleeve of his shirt and lowered his head and painfully started to talk about Camellia.

"Camellia was my best friend and do you know what happened to her?" He raised his bloodshot eyes at Charlie "Her father, a white man, took her away from me. Do you know what he used to do to her? He used to rape her and beat her until she literally bled inside and out. He used to shove things into her, burn her with his cigarette all the way up and down her arms, legs and beat her for not tying her shoelaces properly... She was only ten, Charlie. Only ten." He lowered his head again and let the tears drop down directly to his feet. "Till this day, I have not forgiven myself for letting that happened to her day after day after day. I was her friend. I was supposed to protect her. I should have told someone about it and not kept it a secret. Because of me, she is not here today." Charlie didn't know what to say. He couldn't say anything. He began to feel Gulu's pain and also found himself feeling guilty about his little friend.

"I am sorry," Susan's soft voice came from behind them. Both Gulu and Charlie couldn't look at her. They both looked away from each other and away from her. She stepped in front of Gulu and slowly eased her arms around him and held him close. Her nurturing warm mothering nature made it all the better reason for him to let his feelings and pain flow out onto her shoulder. "I couldn't stop the bleeding . . . I tried to wash it away, but I couldn't stop the bleeding . . ." Gulu cried on Susan's shoulder. The three of them walked back to her house and quietly sat in her living room.

"I am sorry, I should have told you." Charlie's voice was soft and unexpected and Susan and Gulu both looked at him to hear what he had to say. "Ever since your mother and I were kids, I had always been in love with her. When you and your mother came to live with us, I was jealous of you because there was no room for me in her life. I found it hard to accept that the only person, who once gave me all the divided attention, wasn't there for me anymore. She had a son to look after now and there was no room for anyone else in her life. I loved her too much to give up on her that easily. Kungulu, you were everything to her and more. She would have died for you. I had never met a woman quite like her. Strong, beautiful, and spirit driven. She was the kind of person who was always careful with whom she dealt with. I think that's why I loved her. No. I know that's why I love her. She wasn't like other women, you know, insecure; overly dramatic about their lives . . . she was nothing like that. Your mother was something else.

"For the longest time I didn't understand why she was afraid of me. I always tried to force myself into her little world, but my problem was that I was trying too hard. She always had this invisible wall built around her and only certain people were allowed in. When she did let me in, I let her down . . . . ." Charlie began to remember . ... "I let her down." He began to remember that fateful day...

"What do you want from me, huh?" Sarah said angrily.

"I just want to talk, that's all." Charlie said. For the first time in years, Sarah surprised him with the lash of her words.

"Did it not occur to you that I don't want to talk to you, hm? You, a man, would not understand the struggles of a woman. Black or white, we women suffer the same. My child is my happiness and joy, but there isn't a day that goes by that I don't think about how he was brought into this wo'ld. The day you experience rape, you can come and talk to me like a man, not like a boy who is interested in a woman fo' some loving loving." She looked him straight in the eyes with a look that set Charlie afar. She turned back around and continued chopping up the onions on the chopping board. ... He knew better than to say anything. He felt so

bad that he shamefully walked out and did not look back.

"I couldn't face her after that. I didn't know what to say. Say sorry? It wouldn't have been enough. It would have had to take more than just saying sorry. After that, I tried to be more sensitive towards her feelings. I remember when my father kicked me out of the house; she came to me and said…I remember her exact words….. She said, 'you may not be living under your father's roof any more, but you are still of the same blood. You will always be a Bellmont.' She then handed me the little money that she had and told me that everything was going to work out just fine.

"Your mother was always like that. One minute she wouldn't want to have anything to do with me, but the next minute she would be giving me the world. That was when I knew. I knew that this was the woman for me. This was the woman I wanted to spend the rest of my life with. I had known her for twenty years and I was just starting to get to know her.

He reached into his pocket and pulled out his pack of cigarettes. He lit one and took a long drag from it and went back to telling his tale.

"Whenever I knew that my father wasn't home, or was away on business trips for days on end, I used to come and visit her and Catherine as much as I could. Some days I would even get to sleep in my own room, well, now it is changed into the guestroom.

"The first time your mother let me into her world, into her life, I was scared. When she finally gave me the chance, I was scared. I started to see how complicated she was and how foreign she was to me. Me, the man who thought he knew all there was to know about women, was actually afraid to be with one special woman.

"The night before she was arrested at the riots, she had spent the night with me. It was like she knew that something was going to happen to her... Well, it was quite bizarre. It was the first and the last time that I ever shared anything like that with a woman. Half of the night she talked about you, Gulu. I actually started to understand her and myself a little more.

"And then the next day she was gone." He looked down at his hands and at the burning cigarette between his fingers.

Susan reached out for his hand and squeezed it. Here was this stranger, a white man, pouring his heart out. It finally dawned on her that this wasn't about a black woman and a white man. It was about a man and a woman from two different worlds coming together.

"You see, Gulu," Charlie continued "my father disowned me and my mother stood by his side and watched him throw me out of the house. Sarah, who was just somebody who worked for them, gave me all that she had and told me that she believed in me. Nobody has ever done that for me. I want you to understand that I don't want to take her away from you. You are all that she ever lived for. Yes, she loved me, but not as much as she loved you. Hell, what am I talking about? She still loves you. When I saw her the other day, she was dead to the world. She didn't even recognise me. But if she sees you, she will come to life again. Gulu, you are the only one she is hanging on a line for. I don't want her to die without me doing something for her, do you understand?"

Gulu was quiet. He was still thinking about how his mother could have done this to him by loving Charlie. He frowned to himself and gritted his teeth. Charlie looked up at him and waited for him to say something. Anything. Susan looked at the two of them and watched them both carefully. Within the half hour that she had met them, she could see that the connection between them was stronger than they thought. There was something about them that made her want to do something to help them. She cleared her throat and professionally started, "From what it sounds like, time is running out.

What do you want me to do?"

"You mean you will help us get Sarah out of prison?" Charlie had a light spark in his voice. "You …you hardly know us."

"I think I know enough to understand that this woman means a lot to both of you. Now, I will need all the details of Sarah's whereabouts and the history of her arrests if there are any. I also need to have the names of the people who were involved. Give me every detail that you have and try not to leave anything out." As she spoke, Charlie rummaged through his briefcase and pulled out many papers and spread them out on the table and excitedly said, "Well, I can tell you that you will have more than just a case on your hands. This will be a case of a lifetime. The prison that she is in does not even keep records of the prisoners they have there. Some of the prisoners have been there longer than Sarah has. They either live in cramped conditions where they try to fit 30 prisoners in one cell, or they confine them into cubicles much like the one Sarah is in where there is no light and the only ventilation is from the small barred window they have on the door. I could go on and on about this. I have everything on paper. It's all here."

"It looks like you have really done your homework. Okay, what I need right now are just dates and names. Everything else will fall into place."

"I have that list in the car. I'll go get it."Charlie got up and walked out to the car.

"Right. I will just get dressed, if you will excuse me, then we will get to work." Susan also got up and went into the other room to get dressed. When Charlie returned from the car with the rest of his paper work, he found Gulu still sitting in the chair the same way he had left him. His eyes were blood shot from crying earlier on and were fixated on the teacup that was still sitting on the glass coffee table.

"You all right?" Charlie asked him as he rummaged through his paper work on the coffee table.

"Of course I am not all right. What do you expect?" He snapped at him hoarsely. "First you bring me here and then you tell me that you and my mother were lovers? How am I supposed to feel? How the hell am I supposed to act? Do you seriously expect to me to accept it and get on with my life just like that?"

Charlie got up from his couch and went to sit next to Gulu, but Gulu moved further down to the other end of the couch. "Look, I am sorry you had to find out this way, but whether you like it or not, it happened. It wasn't easy for me to say what I said, but it is something that needed to be said."

"Now that you have told me, is it supposed to make me feel better?"

"Oh, grow up, will you?" Charlie got up and went back to his seat on the other couch. "This is as painful for me as it is for you."

"Is it?"

"Look, I am trying. I am really trying. We just have to put our differences aside if you want to see your mother."

"That's easy for you to say." Gulu said painfully. "Well, you are not exactly the easiest person to get

169

along with." He lit another cigarette and turned to his paper work again. They did not say a word to each other until Susan came back looking refreshed and professional in her cream two piece suit.

"Now, what have you got for me?" She sat down by Charlie and glanced at the paperwork he had. "Where did you get all this?" She flipped through a confidential brief composed of names and dates of top police officials and their dealings with the government. On the next page, were names of black officials who were either in exile or were black listed by government. "This is all confidential government material. How did you get hold of this?"

"I've got friends who owe me favours and they have friends who owe them favours all the way to the top. It's not what you know, it's who you know, Ms Kapepe." he gave her an unruly smile.

"We can't use this." She put the papers down on the table. "If we even think about using this documentation in court, it will be their word against ours."

"I am sure you could work something out. You're the lawyer. I am sure there are some legal ways of letting this evidence be exposed to the court."

"You're crazy, you know that? Are you trying to put my career on the line? The only way I play the game is by the rules. You have to remember that this is an all white court and one of me. I have to go by the book, and it is going by the book that has won me cases. I simply give them a taste of their own medicine. Now, if you have something to show me that I can actually use, that you have legally attained, then we will be getting somewhere." Charlie took a deep breath and puffed reluctantly. He went through his briefcase and started pulling out all kinds of other papers that he regretfully put aside.

"What about you Kungulu. Can you tell me about the time your mother was arrested?"

"I don't remember much. There was a lot of tear gas and everything seemed hazy."

"Do you remember the day?" She grabbed her writing pad and started scribbling on it as Gulu talked.

"Yes, it was the day when Ted Tembo came to make a speech in town. Everybody knew about it. It was on the 8th of August, a Thursday. I know it was a Thursday because mama and I used to go into town on Thursdays to see Catherine at the clinic and do a little bit of shopping."

"Do you remember seeing anyone else there? Friends, people you know, maybe?"

"I remember seeing Peter Nkoko, Jason Kabe; . . . I don't remember anyone else."

"Any friends?"
Gulu shook his head helplessly.

"Kungulu, you know that it is important for you to remember as much as possible. What about the police officers who were there?"

"I don't know, it was smoky and my eyes were tearing from the gas, I don't remember." He rubbed his temples and closed his eyes.

"I've got a better idea." Charlie jumped in the middle of the conversation. "Why don't we just go down to the prison and try to take her out?"

"And how do you suppose we are going to do that? Blow down the prison doors?" Gulu said sarcastically.

"Not exactly. Just listen to my plan. It's going to work. Trust me." Charlie's plan was the best plan that they had so far. Susan nervously went along with it and the three of them drove down to the prison. Gulu lay down in the back seat of the car so he could not be seen. Susan and Charlie got out of the car and approached the guard.

"We are here to see Mr Pritchard." Susan Kapepe spoke clearly and professionally.

"And what is this about?" The guard looked her up and down distastefully with a toothpick sticking out from the side of his mouth. Susan pulled out some papers from her case and briefly held them up in the guard's face, then quickly slipped them back in her bag.

"We have a legal document signed by the court for us to see one of your prisoners. Now, if you could so kindly show us to the warden's office, we would like to discuss this with him." She looked him straight in the eyes and did not blink. The guard chewed on his toothpick, and looked at her up and down before looking at Charlie.

"Who is he?" The guard raised his head at Charlie.

"He is with me. If I had it my way, I wouldn't have brought him with me, but the court wants him to accompany me."

"Never trust a blacky," said Charlie with a wry smile. The guard began to smile and said,

"Hey, I remember you. You're the one who got sick last week, eh?

"Yes," Charlie said shamefully, and Susan looked at him surprised.

"You all right now?" the guard asked.

"Yes, thank you. Indigestion." He patted his stomach and avoided looking at Susan.

"Follow me." The guard finally said, and he led them into the prison. Once inside another guard led them to Mr Pritchard's office. When the guard wasn't looking, Susan finally caught Charlie's eye and he knew what she was thinking.

"Once you see the prison cells, you will understand why I got sick." He whispered to her.

"I think I will take your word for it." She stayed close to Charlie's side as they walked down the quiet corridor to Mr Pritchard's office. Mr Pritchard, a tall sturdy older man in his 50's, was a self-affiliated white man who did his work in his own influential way. He kept his paper work in neat piles on his desk and in folders on a wooden shelf in the far corner on the left in his office. He had just become a grandfather today, and he was smoking a cigar by the window. He was staring out far into the land admiring the sun that was just setting over the township not too far from his prison. Ah, how he loved this country. He sucked on his cigar and let the smoke linger in his mouth before slowly blowing it out of his mouth like a mist. He licked his lips and tasted the tobacco soothingly. He then thought about how his wife would throw a fit if she saw him smoking and how he was enjoying every minute of it. Just as he was watching the smoke ascend before him, there was a knock at the door.

"Come," he bellowed.

The guard opened the door for Susan Kapepe and behind her followed Charlie Bellmont.

"Hello, Mr Pritchard. My name is Susan Kapepe." She reached out and firmly shook Mr Pritchard's hand. "I have come here with a court order to inquire about one of your prisoners."

"Why? Is there some sort of problem?"

"There will be if you refuse to co-operate."

"If you don't mind, I would like to see the letter from the court."

Susan pulled out her papers and handed them to Mr Pritchard. He glanced at them and then glanced up at Susan and then at Charlie. He then looked back at the papers and frowned. Susan's heart started to race. It is not going to work, she thought. He is going to arrest us for soliciting legal documents and then he is going to lock us up and throw away the key. She quickly glanced over at Charlie, but he was calm and cool the whole time.

"Who is Sarah Zulu?" Asked Mr Pritchard.

"I am surprised you don't know who she is, Mr Pritchard. She has been in your prison for the past few years, and you are asking us who she is? Don't you have any records of her being transferred here?" Susan was very subtle and Mr Pritchard did not like it. He hated being undermined by a black person let alone, a black woman.

"I must tell you that once prisoners retransferred here, they are not acknowledged by their names, they are given numbers. Names don't mean anything to me. If you have a serial number for this certain individual, I will give you a whole history on her if you like." He glared at Susan and right off, he knew he didn't like her.

"Mr Pritchard, I am sure you remember me," Charlie said.

"Yes, I remember you Mr . . ."

"Bellmont, sir."

"Bellmont. I may have forgotten your name, but I never forget a face. You were the one who was quite interested in Singing Gabrielle. Yes, that's what we call her, the Singing Gabrielle. Might she be the one you are looking for?" Number 4449214?"

"Yes, quite so." Charlie replied.

"Well, correct me if I am wrong, but usually when we get legal documents inquiring about our prisoners, they always have their serial number somewhere on their paper work, but yours doesn't. According to me, this piece of paper is not worth anything to me." He dangled the piece of paper before them as he held it between his index finger and thumb before he let it go and they all watched it cascade down onto his desk.

"Mr Pritchard, that piece of paper is as genuine as your job. If you do not meet our needs, you will have to hear it from Judge Rollins and believe me, if you think you can disregard his request, he can disregard your job faster than you could blink. Do you understand where we are coming from, sir?" Susan's palms were clammy. "If you really want to hear the request from the judge himself, you can always call him." She added.

"But I wouldn't do that if I were you," Charlie added quickly. "He is a very bitter man who hates petty phone calls. But if you must, and you feel confident enough to risk your job by interrupting his teatime, please, go ahead. I didn't want to come down here again, but he gave me no choice. I didn't want to argue with him myself."

Mr Pritchard looked at them both and thought about what they had just said. He then thought about his wife and her medical bills he still had to pay. He looked over the document and then sat down in his big black leather chair. He put his cigar down and evidently had no taste for it anymore. "All right. I will have one of my guards take you to her cell and I will fill out her release forms, which you will have to sign."

"Well, I knew we would come to an understanding." Charlie gave his boyish smile, but he knew that they were not in the clear yet. Mr Pritchard called for a guard to show them to Sarah's cell. When they walked through the halls, the nature of the prison was sombre and dull, just as Charlie remembered them.

175

Being in there again sent a chill down his spine and he became afraid again. Susan took out her handkerchief and covered her mouth from the musty odour of stale urine that lingered in the air.

The guard opened the door to Sarah's cell where she was curled up in the corner inattentively. The cell was only big enough for one other person to go in. Charlie walked through and cupped Sarah's cheek with his trembling clammy hands. She was ice cold. He patted her cheeks to see if she would wake up, but she didn't. Immediately, he knew that there was something wrong. In haste, he scooped her up in his arms and carried her out.

"Is she okay?" Susan asked, still covering her mouth with her handkerchief.

"No. She is ice cold. We need to get her to a hospital." Charlie raced down the hall and realised he didn't know how to get out of there. "Bloody hell, man. Show us the way out of this prison." He barked at the guard. The guard picked up his pace and led them through the winding halls and out to the front gate where their car was parked. As he locked the gate, he watched Susan open the back door for Charlie and it was at that moment he noticed somebody else was sitting up in the back seat. He quickly unlocked the gate, but it was too late. They had already sped off down the gravel road towards the township. The guard ran back into the prison and into Mr Pritchard's office. Just when he barged into the office without knocking, Mr Pritchard slammed down the phone and was infuriated. "Where are they?" He barked.

"They just left, sir. I tried to stop them, but they got away. I knew there was something going on when I saw that coloured boy in the back seat of their car. I tried to stop them, but they drove off too quickly."

"Damn!" Mr Pritchard got to his feet and pulled out a file from his wooden shelf and flipped through it vigorously. He ran down pages with his forefinger through the names of judges and did not see a Judge Rollins. He scanned through the page again and still did not see anything familiar. In a rage, he flung the folder to the floor sending papers cascading around his office. He had been conned and one of his prisoners had escaped. In the car, Gulu sat in the back seat holding his mother in his arms calling out to her, "Mama, mama, please mama, can you hear me?"

Charlie sped down the street and around the corners frantically. He kept looking in his rear view mirror at Gulu holding Sarah. Charlie became scared. He couldn't lose her now. There was so much he wanted to tell her.

When they arrived at St. Joseph's Hospital, Charlie pulled up in the emergency entrance only marked for ambulances.

"Charlie, they are not going to treat her here. This is an all whites' hospital."

"The hell they're not!" He yelled. He climbed out of the driver's seat and opened the back seat door and took Sarah in his arms and carried her into the hospital yelling, "Please, somebody help me!" The nurses in their white caps and the doctors in their white coats, stopped to look at him. Even the patients with their walkers and those in wheel chairs, stopped to look at this man who had just barged in with a black woman in his arms. Nobody took a step towards him. "Please! Somebody, I need a doctor!" He yelled again. As he made his way to the front desk, everyone stepped away from him. The receptionist and the nurses who stood behind the counter could not believe what they were seeing.

"You're a nurse, get me a doctor." He said to one ofthem.

"Get that thing out of here!" Said the nurse disgusted.

"This person that you call a thing is a human being just like you and I. Now get me a doctor, now!"

"Sir, if you don't leave now, I will have to call security."

"Jesus Christ! What do I have to do to get a doctor around here?" Charlie walked down the reception area with Sarah still unconscious in his arms. The nurse dialled for security and before Charlie could make it around the corner, a security guard stopped him.

"Hey, where do you think you are going with that black woman in a white hospital?"

"To find a doctor who will treat her."

"I am sorry, but I am going to have to ask you to take your patient somewhere else. This is an all white hospital. No niggers allowed." Charlie carefully placed Sarah down on the cold marble floor and then pulled out his gun from the back of his trousers. The people around him gaped and ducked down close to the ground. He held the gun to the guard's face and gritted his teeth,

"If you don't find me a doctor who will help her, I will blow your cheek off and the janitor will spend the rest of his afternoon cleaning the pieces of your face off the wall."

"Charlie," Susan's shaking voice came from behind him. "...you don't have to do this. There is another hospital just as good not too far from here that will treat Sarah."

"No!" He yelled. "We are here, and they are going to give her the best treatment they have!"

"Charlie, listen to me!"

"No, you listen! I have had it up to here!" He pressed the gun against the guard's cheek as if he was about to fire. Everyone held their breath in and hoped he wouldn't do the unthinkable.

"Charlie!" Gulu yelled at him and marched towards him. "Don't be stupid, man. You're wasting your time here. Even if you do get these white people to treat her, what makes you think they are going to give her the best care they have? She is black, not white. Put your stupid gun away and we will take her to another place where we know she will get the help she needs!" He then bent down to his mother who was still lying unconscious on the cold floor, and struggled to pick her up. Charlie put his gun away and helped Gulu carry her to the car. Gulu angrily narrowed his eyes at him and then muttered, "Stupid," at him and then sucked his teeth. Charlie was too much in a panic that he did as he was told and got in the car sped down the road to the other side of town to a black hospital.

Once they got her into the intensive care unit, Charlie slowly, but surely started to get himself together. They sat in the waiting room knowing that all they could do now was wait.

"What the hell came over you, man?" Gulu surveyed.

"I don't know. I guess I just panicked." He ran his fingers through his hair and thought about what had come over him. "I just panicked." His voice cracked. He went outside to have a smoke and when he returned, he still looked distressed.

The doctor came back to let them know that they could see her. He explained to them that she had pneumonia and was suffering from dehydration.

"Fortunately, we were able to stabilise her. The unfortunate thing about her condition is that the infection

179

that had developed in the open wound above her eye has spread to the cornea, covering the pupil. We could try to surgically remove the infection over the pupil, but it doesn't guarantee that she will get her sight back. As for her right hand, the nerve endings in some of her fingers have been damaged. There is nothing we can do to get any feeling back in her finger. She will have to be hospitalised for a couple more days. There are still a few more tests I want to run, and I want to make sure she is in top condition before she leaves the hospital." He took a deep breath and lightly added, "The good news is that she is not allergic to penicillin and it's helping her recover much quicker. She is still very weak. You can only see her for a few minutes."

"Why don't the both of you go see her? I will wait here for you." Susan insisted. Charlie and Gulu walked in her room and they both stood by on either side of her bed and looked down at her.

"I can't believe she is actually here." Gulu said softly and he gently stroked her forehead with the tips of his fingers.

"I know." Charlie agreed.

They both studied her pallid face that had aged drastically over the years. Her skin had become rough and leathery, her swollen shut eye and chapped lips gave a new impression of who she had become. Despite her extenuated altered features Sarah still looked beautiful. She was still the same person underneath the wounds.

"Charlie, I ...." Gulu didn't know how to say it. His mouth hung open as he tried to choose the right words. Finally, he said, "Thank you. Mama wouldn't be here if it wasn't for you." He couldn't look at Charlie.

"I was only doing what was right." He said looking at him. For the first time in a long time, he felt complete. The weight that once weighed him down on the inside disappeared and his heart pulsated and set itself afloat.

"But I also want to let you know that I still hate you, you know." Charlie smiled at him and Gulu answered,

"I know. I still hate you too." Gulu bent down and placed his lips on his mother's forehead and just at that moment, he felt her eyes twitch.

"Mama," he said. "Mama," he called out to her again. Her lips moved and a hoarse, but faint voice came out.

"The sky," she said.
"What did she say?" Charlie asked and leaned in close to hear what she was saying.

"The sky," she repeated dryly. "African Skies..." she said dragging the last word out before she drifted out of consciousness. Gulu called out to her again and tried to wake her, but she was out again. Just then, Susan abruptly came into the room.

"They're here." She said nervously.
"Who?" Charlie asked.
"Mr Pritchard and one of his men. They didn't see me, but I saw and heard them asking about us at the reception."

"What are we going to do?" Gulu panicked.
"They won't let white people up here just to take a sick patient back to prison." Susan tried to reassure them.

"How do you know? I am white and they let me come in." said Charlie.

"That's different. You brought in a black patient. You weren't here to arrest one. Quickly, we must get out of here."

"What about mama? I am not leaving without her." Gulu insisted.

"Don't worry, Gulu. I just talked to the doctor and he said he will look after her . . ."

"No, I am not leaving her here alone." He blurted out.

"Gulu, trust me. They can't touch her here. These are our grounds and because she is in critical condition, they are not stupid enough to arrest her and have her die in their custody."

"No." Gulu said firmly.

"Gulu, she's right," assured Charlie. "Even if they did try to take her, the people in this hospital will not let them walk out of here alive." Gulu thought for a moment as he looked at his mother lying unconscious on the bed. He hated the way things had turned out, but he had to do what needed to be done. He kissed her again on the forehead and swallowed hard at the thought of being parted from her again.

"Okay." Gulu finally said. "Let's go." One of the nurses showed them down the stairs and through the back entrance of the hospital. Outside, there was an ambulance waiting for them to take them to their next destination.

"Why are they all helping us?" asked Charlie.

"Unlike white people, we have a tendency to stick together through thick and thin. Kind of like a marriage.....till death do us part." explained Susan. That remark hit home for Charlie and took the comment personally, but he ignored it and push it to the back of his mind.

When the ambulance stopped wailing and the engine was turned off, they climbed out and found themselves in poverty stricken black neighbourhood. The place was congested with small clay houses separated by narrow alleys and small streams of polluted water that divided their homes. Malnourished chickens ran around their miniature court yards, ragged clothing hung on strings of rope to dry in the gentle zephyr that blew smoke in their direction from a small fire made outside one of the homes.

"Where are we?" asked Charlie as he looked around the estranged place.

"Katongo Township." Said Susan. She inhaled deeply and then exhaled loudly. "I love this place." she smiled remembering the familiar odours and scents that floated aimlessly in the air. She thanked the driver and then led Gulu and Charlie to one of the clay houses. "Hodi?" She called out as she pushed the long woven drapery that covered the entrance.

"Kalibu," answered a frail voice from inside. An old lady limped to the door and with bright eyes and open arms, she greeted Susan. "Kookoo, baby." and hugged her close.

"Buya, mami. Muli bwanji?" Susan and her great aunt started conversing in a dialect that neither Charlie nor Gulu understood. Gulu was able to pick up a few familiar words, but not enough to understand what they were saying. Susan introduced her friends and with them not expecting it, she greeted them with a warm hug and a kiss on the cheek.

"You will stay with her tonight until tomorrow morning." Susan explained to them. "This is the safest place I could think of and I know they will not come here looking for you."

"What about you? Aren't you going to stay with us?" Gulu asked.

"Don't worry about me. I will just be a couple of houses down at my granny's house. There isn't enough space here for all of us. As it is, you two will have to share a bed. I will see you two in the morning at the crack of dawn. Sleep well." And she was gone. Although Susan's great aunt was old, she was able to make them a full African meal in her little courtyard. She sat on a small wooden stool and cooked over a small fire that she had made earlier on that afternoon. Charlie and Gulu watched hungrily as the aroma of the cooking filtered their nostrils. She fried some beef with onions and tomatoes and then left it to simmer in its own juices. She then replaced the pan with another small round pot, which she used to boil some salted green vegetables. When the greens were ready, she then put that pot aside and put a larger one in its place filled with water. Once the water boiled, she poured some ground corn meal in it. As the corn meal began to splatter, she added some more of the crushed grains andmechanically churned it with a wooden spoon until it cooked into a white paste. Gulu had seen this done many times by his mother day after day, and later learned to cook it for himself. But Charlie was seeing the whole preparation for the first time. He knew that it was the black people's staple diet, but he never bothered to pay attention and how it was made from scratch.

She dished out the Nshima with a wooden spoon and neatly patted it on a plate. She dished out the meat and vegetable into small bowls and set them on a mat on the floor where they sat to eat. Susan's great aunt and Gulu showed Charlie how to roll the Nshima into a ball in his hand and dip it in the gravy and scoop the meat with it. The few times he had eaten it, he had used a fork. Reluctantly, he mimicked Gulu and Susan's great aunt. Unsuccessfully, juices dribbled down his chin, along his arm and failed to tempt to master eating Nshima. In all the years that Charlie had been living in

Africa, this was his first full traditional African meal he ever had and he enjoyed every minute of it.

After dinner, she did the cleaning up and also made their bed. When Charlie offered to help, she refused and Gulu explained to him that she would be offended if he even tried to lift a finger. When the moon was full and the stars formed the constellations in the sky, she was already fast asleep in her bed. Gulu lay down restlessly on the bed while Charlie sat outside in the cool night smoking a cigarette.

"Can't sleep?" Gulu startled him.

"No," he replied honestly. Gulu sat down next to him on the ground and watched Charlie take another drag from his cigarette and inhale deeply before exhaling through his nose and mouth. "Would you like one?" He offered.

Gulu shook his head and crinkled his face.

"I don't smoke." He said. He continued watching Charlie as he started blowing little rings of smoke out of his mouth. "How do you do that?" Gulu asked in amazement. Charlie smiled amusingly and handed Gulu his half-smoked cigarette.

"Here, try it."

Gulu perked his lips and put the cigarette to his mouth and inhaled just as he had seen Charlie do. He felt the rush of toxins go down his windpipe and burn his chest. His eyes started to water and he coughed frantically to get the smoke out of his chest. Charlie laughed and tried to help him by patting him on his back.

"That's why you shouldn't smoke." He laughed. "Are you okay?"

Still coughing and his eyes tearing endlessly, Gulu nodded. When he finally recovered from his attack, they sat quietly listening to the quiet night. An evening chill crept by them and made the hairs on Gulu's arm stand. He pulled his knees in to keep himself warm and looked up to the sky. Studying it, he then finally said, "Charlie, what do you think mama was trying to say in the hospital?"

"African skies." He replied and also looked up to the dark sky.

"I know that that is what she said, but what did she mean?"

"She means just that. The African skies." Gulu looked at him little confused. "Don't you know the legend of the African skies?" Charlie asked him.

"All Africans, black and white should know about their own African skies. Our skies never lie. They are always telling the truth. You see, many, many years ago, when our forefathers, yours and mine, always used the sky for guidance. Whether the sun was up or the moon was full, it meant something. Sometimes they predicted wars, sometimes they predicted peace. Sometimes even love if you looked hard enough at the stars. Like tonight for example. The moon is full; stars are shining.....that is telling us that everything is in sequence. It is going in a steady flow. If you are in love, you will see your lover's face in the moon. But if there is lightning, thunder and heavy storms, something terrible is supposed to happen. Maybe death, war, destruction...I don't know. It depends. One thing is for sure. Our skies never lie. They tell us the truth about ourselves. If we are going in the wrong direction in life, our paths would be filled with storms and thunder. If we are going in the right direction in life, the sun will shine brighter than ever, and at night the moon will glow bright enough for us to see where we are going in the dark. And the stars, like ancient navigators, will show you the way." Charlie continued with a smile on his face.

"My grandfather told my father and my father told me about our great skies. There is nowhere in the world that the skies tell as many stories as they do in Africa. As Africans, we should be proud and never forget.

"It's kind of like mother earth. She is the giver of life, but she cannot do it without the rains or sunlight. The African skies give us life, and can damn well take it back."

Gulu sat and thought about the logistics of the African Skies. He looked up at the sky again and thought about what Charlie had just said. The North Star winked at him repeatedly and the grey shadows that formed the surface of the moon seemed more eloquent than before. Then he remembered a song that his mother used to sing to him about the sun chasing the moon, but would never ever catch up to it. The sun would always be right behind the moon shining and shadowing its surface. The African skies made him begin to understand his dreams and visions of his mother. A sense of clarity came over him and he felt more comfortable. He went back into the shack and slept soundly and did not wake till morning.

That morning, Susan had come for them at the crack of dawn just as she had promised. They gathered their things and went back to the hospital. When they arrived at the hospital, they were taken through the back entrance and up the stairs to Sarah's room. She lay in bed and was vacantly looking out her window watching the sunrise. Charlie and Gulu rushed to her side. She looked at them blankly, not recognising who they were. She then turned her head back to the window and continued watching the sunrise.

"We have to hurry," said Susan. "…the whole police force is looking for you and the only way to get away from them is to go underground for a while. I have some friends who can help you. But first, we have to get Sarah out of here. Quickly, Charlie. Can you lift her up?"

Charlie slipped his arms underneath Sarah and gently cradled her in his arms.

"Where are we going?" He asked.

"Back to the truck. Follow me." Charlie and Gulu followed close behind her back down the stairs and out the back entrance and into the same truck they came in on. Gulu huddled close to Charlie who sat holding Sarah in his lap. The half hour bumpy ride that seemed like forever finally came to an end. They climbed out and found themselves in a warehouse.

"Quickly," ordered Susan. Another man came out of a small office in the corner of the warehouse and handed Susan a large manila envelope. She hugged the man and thanked him.

"What's going on?" Charlie was getting nervous now.

"You are going underground for a while." explained the man. Susan opened the envelop and said,

"And these are your new passports and,"

"Hold up, just a minute. What do you mean new passports? As far as I know about going underground, you don't get new passports, your existence is deleted. Now, what's the deal with the passports? Are we going somewhere?" Susan looked at the man who handed her the passports and they both knew that they had to explain to them what was really going on. "You, Kungulu and Sarah are going out of the country for a while. Sarah needs medical care, and in such cases like this, we always try to get people out of the country to get the treatment. Now, please, there is no time. We are switching trucks now and I will explain the rest on the way."

"No, I am not taking another step until you tell me what is going on and where we are going." demanded Charlie. Susan and the man looked at each other and Susan began to explain again.

"Charlie, the whole police force is looking for you. They know who you are, they know where you live and they will not stop until they find you. When they do find you, they will kill you before you even try to explain yourself. This is what Black Listed means. Now, the best way to keep you guys alive is to take you out of the country for a couple of years and then return when things have cooled down."

"Where would we go?"

"Northern Rhodesia."

"What about England. At least I know my way around there."

"Too expensive. We only have enough to get you across the border not fly you out."

"I can afford it. I have enough money in my savings." Charlie thought for a second and then said, "Could you excuse Gulu and me for a second?" Susan agreed and she walked towards the other truck with the other man.

"Listen to me Gulu, I don't think your mother is going to make the long trip. She is still too weak."

"I know," Gulu droned in his words.

"My suggestion is to go to Catherine. That is, me and Sarah."

"You filthy snake!" Gulu started to swing his fists at him furiously and Charlie tried to get a hold of him.

"Listen to me before you lose your top!"
Charlie stopped him and gripped his wrists firmly and looked Gulu straight in the eyes and did not blink.

"I am getting old and I have no business in England. You do. You are still young; you can make something of yourself."

"What the hell am I supposed to do in a foreign country by myself?"

"Go to school. Do your "A" levels, go to college and make something of yourself because this country has got nothing for you. Once everything has calmed down here, then you can start thinking about coming back."

"No. I am not going alone. Either you or mama comes with me or I don't go. You said it yourself. Mama is weak. She needs all the medical aid she can get. Why not get that medical aid in England? You need to come along because you know England better than I do." Charlie looked into Gulu frightened and insecure eyes and finally gave in.

"Okay, okay. I will come with you. But I will only be there for a few weeks to get you settled into a good school and Sarah settled with good medical help, then I am coming back."

"Why? Why don't you also stay and make a new life in England?""Because this is my home and I have no business in England."

"What are you going to do when you come back?"

"Stay with Catherine for a while, and I am going to keep trying to patch things up with my parents. I am done with my criminal life. I have washed my hands in it."

"Please, we have to hurry." Susan's voice echoed across the warehouse.

"Just a minute." Charlie echoed back. "So, how about it? Shall we shake on it?" He stuck out his hand

and Gulu hesitated for a moment before shaking it. He didn't know why, but he trusted Charlie this time.

They climbed into the other truck and told Susan about their new plan. She assured them that they would still have to cross the border into Rhodesia, and if they still wanted to fly to England, they could do so from there. It would be too risky to try and fly out of Mtesa.

"Before we hit the border, I will need to go to the bank and withdraw my money." said Charlie. Twenty minutes had gone by and the truck finally stopped and was parked in an alley about three blocks from the bank.

"I guess this is where I get off then." Charlie climbed out of the truck looking both ways as he started to close the back door of the truck.

"Charlie," Susan called out to him. "…be careful." she said looking worried. He smiled and winked at her before he disappeared behind the corner of another street. Right when he put a cigarette to his lips, three black schoolboys ran towards him. One of them stopped to pick up a stone and throw it at the police officers behind them. Without waiting to see if they hit the police officers, they ran passed Charlie almost knocking him down. From a distance, he heard a gunshot and sirens followed by screams. At that moment, a stampede of people started coming in his direction and more gunshots were fired. The mob that ran past him were school children who were either Gulu's age or younger. One of the schoolboys stopped and spat at him square in the face and yelled at him, "Foosek!" and ran ahead with the rest of his school mates.

"What the hell is going on?" he wiped the spittle off his face with the sleeve of his shirt. He got to the bank and saw the closed sign hanging on the glass door. He pressed his face against the window and saw the people inside frantically getting their things together.

He knocked on the window to get their attention, but they all ignored him and kept on doing whatever they were doing. He knocked again and waved his hand at a woman who glanced up in his direction. He knocked again and she looked around her making sure that nobody in the bank was watching before she made her way to the door. She unlocked the door and opened it enough to stick her head out.

"Mr Belmont, what are you doing here? Go home. It is not safe for you to be out in the streets now."

"What the hell is going on around here? I almost got trampled on by a mob of school kids." He could tell that her nerves were on the edge when she spoke. "Didn't you hear? Ted Tembo was just shot and the people have been going crazy."

"What? Who shot him?"

"I don't know . . . look, I must go. We are going to be closed until the riots are over." She began to close the door, but he was quick to put his foot in the door.

"Wait, I need to withdraw some money. I am going out of town today. In fact, right this minute. Please, just let me come in and make the transaction. It will only be a minute." He gave her a pleading eye, which he knew she could not turn away.

"Okay, Mr Belmont, but we will have to be quick." She opened the door enough for him to slip through, and quickly shut it with the bolt. When he withdrew all his savings and she closed his account, he placed a wet kiss on her cheek and charmed her,

"You are the best, Caroline." and was gone. Back in the truck, Susan was getting nervous. She could hear the sound of gun shots and people yelling and screaming from a distant and she wondered whether Charlie was caught up in the commotion. "Where the hell is he?" Just as she said that, Charlie startled them when he pulled the back door open. He climbed in banged on the wall of the truck and yelled to the driver to go. "Let's go, let's go! Let's get the hell out of here!" The engine roared and jerked as it started down the street in the opposite direction of the riot. He sat next to Sarah who was slouching over Gulu's shoulder. He pulled her onto his lap and breathlessly began to explain. "Ted Tembo has just been shot." "Oh my God..." Susan's eyes uncontrollably flooded with tears and Gulu stared at Charlie in shock. His mouth hung open and could not believe that his hero, his freedom fighting idol, was dead. Charlie continued to explain. "The lady in the bank told me. He was giving a speech in the middle of town at King Edward Circle when he got shot. She said that it only happened a little while before we got here and when the crowd got wild and crazy after he got shot, all the shopkeepers started closing the stores and the police were firing bullets in every direction. She told me that there were some school children that had come on a school trip to hear him speak. And as I was trying to get back to the truck, a schoolgirl ran by me and then next thing I knew, she was shot dead in the back. For a second there I thought the policeman was going to shoot me, but he ran passed me and aimed and shot another schoolboy. I don't know. I don't know anymore." He shivered. For the next four hours they road in silence as they left the disordered city behind them. Susan huddled in the corner by herself and felt like her whole world had just crumbled from underneath her. Now that the man who was going to lead her people to freedom was dead, who was going to do it?

The truck stopped and the driver climbed out and came around back to open the back door. "We rest

now and eat. We start again when the sun goes down."
He told them.

It was almost dark and they had stopped in a deserted spot by the narrow dirt road that stretched out on far ahead and continued through the savannah grasslands and disappeared to what seemed like the edge of the earth. They made a small fire and had a simple meal of tea and bread with butter. Gulu and Susan were not very hungry. They mournfully sat sipping their tea quietly. Gulu was sitting under a tree with his mother's head resting on his thigh, and Susan was sitting on a rock overlooking the savannah grasslands, watching the sun disappear behind what seemed like the edge of the earth. Charlie came up from behind her and placed a blanket over her shoulders and sat down next to her.

"Thank you." Her voice was hoarse.

"I love this country." He breathed out the words in a sigh. "You can do anything and be anybody you want, because it's got so much to offer." Like Susan, his eyes stared out into the open country of savannah.

"No, you can do anything." She emphasised and corrected him. "*You* can do what *you* want, and *you* can be anybody *you* want to be. Not us."

Drivelled with guilt, Charlie did not look at her. With his one foot, he drew half circles in the dirt and quickly changed the subject.

"Can I ask you something? Why are you doing this?" He continued drawing half circles in the dirt. Knowing what he meant, she turned away from the horizon and looked at him.

"Why?" She echoed his question. "The answer is simple. He is sitting over there." She motioned with a nod towards Gulu and his mother. "That boy, like many other black and coloured boys, has potential

194

once he is given the chance. But the only thing that is holding him back is the stupid system of ours, which blatantly destroys his chances in life. As a lawyer, I have lost cases where I have seen children like him and younger be tortured and killed for some senseless reason by their parents or people they know. They don't give a damn about their children. If they don't, then who will? It is hard, you know." Her hoarse voice quivered, "I know all their names, their faces . . . . . their faces which I can never forget. My mother always used to be angry with me because I would spend sleepless nights trying to prepare myself for each case and then I would lose." She smiled as she remembered. "She always used to say to me, you can't save all their lives at once! One at a time. . . . one at a time."

"And that is exactly what you are doing." He put his arm around her shoulders and she rested her head on his shoulder and they both looked out into the silhouette of the tall grasses as the sun eventually disappeared below the earth.

"What are you going to do when you get back?"

"I don't know. Keep working . . . . Maybe retire and write a book about my work, I don't know. All I know is that I am tired."

"I don't think it will be safe for you back there. If they are looking for us, as you say, then they are bound to come looking for you." He looked at her with concern.

"Don't worry about me. I can take care of myself. I always have." She reassured him.

"I don't know," He doubted her. "it looked like a revolution was starting up back there. I think we will be hiding out in London for a while before coming back. I feel kind of funny about it, though. I feel as though we are running away from our own problems."

"You are not running away. You are trying to save a young boy and his mother's life."

"You know what? This time last year I would have never thought of taking out all my life savings and spending it on Gulu. I have always been selfish."

"People change. You have changed, because you have a common trait. Sarah."

"I would do anything for her." He turned to look at Susan and added, "I have loved her for as long as I can remember, but you know what the sad thing about this whole thing is? I am not doing it for Gulu. I am doing this for her because it would have been what she wanted." He quickly looked back out into the fields hoping she didn't see the sensitivity and guilt in his face. "I guess I am still doing something that will make me happy and not Gulu. I guess I haven't changed much, have I?"

"That just proves that you are human. Love can make you do things and not know why you are doing them."

"Okay!" The driver yelled out. "Let's go! We have to try and get to the border before sunrise!" They gathered up their things and climbed back into the truck. The ride was vigorous and uncomfortable. Susan, Charlie and the driver took shifts in driving until they reached the border where the river separates Graceland from Rhodesia. It was 2:30 in the morning and the moonlight was the only light to be seen. "I hope you can swim." said the driver. "You are going to have to take that little boat over there and paddle to the other side. Remember to keep your hands and feet in the boat because the crocodiles will snap at anything that moves."

"Why can't we just go to the border?" asked Charlie.

"Because they are most possibly waiting for people like you at the border so they could send you back."

"He is right, Charlie." Said Susan.

They all got out of the truck and stared out across the black water to the dark bushes that hung over the edge of the bank. The water was calm, but the humidity rose with the sound of crickets and the hippos mating calls reverberating in the dark. The only light that came from the moon shadowed the rustling night creatures in the bushes. The moon reflected on the water and formed silver streaks across the surface. Gulu and Charlie nervously climbed into the boat with Sarah. Almost in a whisper, Susan leaned into the boat and said to them,

"Remember, there will be a man waiting for you on the other side. He is expecting you. His name is Peter Smith. He is an Englishman who has helped us for many years. If he is not there, stay there and wait for him. Do not go anywhere. Don't try to find him. He will find you. Here are your passports. You may not need them, but they were made just in case." Susan handed Charlie the envelope and then hugged them both goodbye. As they drifted off towards the middle of the river, she whispered loudly, "Be careful and good luck." Charlie and Gulu started to paddle to the other side. Just as they were crossing, the reflection of the moon in the middle of the river gave way for other men hiding in the bush to see them. A gunshot was fired and a bullet splashed in the water right by where Gulu was paddling. Voices were heard yelling and more shots were being fired. Charlie and Gulu peddled faster and Susan and the driver watched helplessly as they saw them being showered by bullets.

"Aaah!" howled Charlie. He fell back into the boat gripping his arm.

"Charlie!" Gulu screamed. He stopped paddling and fell into the boat to check if Charlie was all right.

"Keep paddling, I will be all right." Charlie groaned in pain.

"I can't . . ." Gulu lay on top of him paralysed. Susan and the driver had seen Charlie get shot and then saw Gulu go down. There was nothing that they could do.

"Let's go!" The driver dragged Susan by the arm towards the truck.

"No, wait." She jerked her arm away from him.

"We can't. We have to go. There is nothing that we can do for them." He pushed her into the truck and as they started to drive off, she pleaded with him as she was almost in tears.

"Stop! Please, just for a minute. I know they are going to make it." The driver stopped the truck and they both looked behind them through their windows and they kept their eyes on the boat in the middle of the river.

"Get up and paddle!" Yelled Charlie.

"I can't . . ." Gulu was now crying hysterically. His whole body was shaking and his teeth were chattering. He was gripping onto Charlie's shirt tightly when he felt the bullets whiz over his head and splash into the water.

"Get up, damn you! Get up!" Charlie screamed at him. Gulu couldn't stop crying. "Gulu, get up! If you don't paddle and get us out of here, we will die!" With his trembling hands, Gulu picked up his paddle and started paddling and kept his body low. On the other side of the bank, somebody was firing bullets to the perpetrators who were firing at the boat. The crossfire continued and Gulu kept paddling while streams of tears ran down his face.

"Faster! Paddle faster!" Somebody yelled from the other side of the bank. From behind the thick greenery that bowed to the surface of the water, Gulu could see a man signalling to him to paddle faster. Gulu focused on him and kept paddling until the boat hit the bank. The man grabbed the boat and pulled it up onto the bank into the bushes.

When Susan saw that the boat had reached the other side of the river, she turned to the driver and said,

"Let's go. We can go now." She sighed in relief and for the first time in 36 hours, she closed her eyes and could feel her body relaxing into a deep sleep.

Back at the bank, Peter Smith, a burly English man with a red beard helped them out of the boat and as soon as they disappeared into the dark bushes, the gun shots which were being fired at them from the other side stopped. They climbed up the steep muddy hill to his jeep which was camouflaged in the bushes.

"I was expecting you yesterday. Are you all right mate?" He said to Charlie.

"I will be all right." Charlie winced as he applied pressure with his hand on his wound and tried to stop the bleeding. "How is Sarah?" he asked as he turned to Gulu.

"She's okay," Gulu's voice was trembling, but he was now starting to calm down. Sarah's face was still as vacant as it was earlier on. She had not spoken a word and she did not flinch or react to all the commotion in the middle of the river. It worried Gulu that she was not responding to her surroundings, but he kept his thoughts to himself.

"Now this is what's going to happen." The burley Englishman began to explain. "We are going to get you a full medical check-up and then we will have you on a plane to England. It's not much of a plane, it's filled with cargo. I hope you have your new passports, because we don't have time to get you new ones now. You won't need them here, but you will need them once you get to England. We only have until the sun sets and that is in four hours." "Gulu, give me my bag." said Charlie. Gulu handed him their only piece of luggage which consisted of Charlie's life savings wrapped in a plastic bag with a rubber band around it, and the manila envelope with their passports in it. Charlie pulled out the manila envelope and gave it to Gulu. "Open it." he ordered him. Gulu opened the envelope and pulled out three British passports. Gulu flipped through one and stopped to study the picture in it.

"I think this is you." Almost laughing he held the passport in front of Charlie's face so he could see. Charlie looked at the name David Robert Collins and above that was a picture of a blond and blue eyed man with a long narrow nose and sunken cheekbones.

"This doesn't look like me. This man looks like a bloody pompous ass." He said irritated.

"If you think yours is bad, look at mine." Gulu disgustingly held his passport in Charlie's face. Charlie looked at a picture of a chubby green-eyed coloured boy named David Coolbear. Charlie and Gulu looked at each other and started to laugh. Charlie turned to Smith and chuckled,

"We're not seriously going to use these passports, are we?"

"Of course we are. You have to remember that you have been given new names with new identities. All that is left to do is replace those pictures with yours. That won't take long. We can do that once we get to the airport." "I hope so, because we don't look a thing like these people." Charlie commented and felt a sudden rush of pain go through him from his arm. When they got to Smith's lodge, there was another man there who dressed Charlie's wound. When they were cleaned up, they took new pictures and the professionals they were, they replaced the old pictures with the new ones. On their way to the airport, they had a flat tyre, which put them even more behind schedule. By the time they got to the landing strip, they saw that it was in the middle of nowhere. When they got on the plane, the engine of the jumbo jet cargo rumbled and they were ready for take-off. There were four other black men who were flying out with them. The plane loudly roared down the runway and finally ascended into the sky. Through conversation, Gulu and Charlie learned that the other passengers were also from Graceland. They were black listed activists who were also running for their lives. Gulu then explained to them that Ted Tembo had just been shot and then one of them mournfully replied,

"I will never return to my country until my people are free. That is a promise."

"Then you will be waiting for a long time, my friend." Commented the other man. As they soared through the mist and white clouds, Gulu looked out a small window and watched as the sun was just beginning to set. He pulled his mother closer and turned her head to the light.

"Look mama, look how beautiful Africa is from up here." They watched the day come to life. The transparent orange and yellow hue rays filtered through the grasslands down below. A miniature heard of giraffes galloped together towards east. The earth seemed to move as the clouds floated in front of their window and just then, the sun shown right in Sarah's face. Her eyes lit up and she came to life.

"My Africa," She said. Taken by surprise, Charlie turned to look at her and couldn't believe what he had just heard. "Afreeeca," She repeated with glowing eyes as she stared out into the sunlight and floating clouds. Gulu smiled with tears filling his eyes.

"Yes, mama. Your Africa, your home." He cried. Charlie watched her beam at the sight outside the plane and his eyes grew with love for her once again.

"My Afreeeeca!" She repeated this time with a smile. "Africa." She said softer. "Africa."

Chapter Eight

Susan inserted her keys into her front door and could not wait to kick off her shoes and put her feet up. She had been gone for three days and three nights and all she could think of now was sleep. She threw herself on her couch and closed her eyes. She felt her body sink through the cushions as she began to drift off into a deep sleep, but she suddenly couldn't breathe. Her neck became tight and began to burn as she felt something press against her neck and block her windpipe. She opened her eyes and saw him. She began to struggle and fight for her life. She waved her arms and like a wild cat, she scratched his face. Stunned, he picked her up by her neck and dragged her onto the coffee table and straddled her. She fought again, but he grabbed onto her arms and pinned them above her head. She tried to scream, but her voice came out hoarse. Why was he doing this to her? What was he doing in her house? Her eyes became wide with terror when she saw him raise a knife above his head. A wild scream finally came out of her right before he brought it down into her left shoulder. He twisted the knife and then pulled it out and held it above his head again. His flaming mad eyes changed with unsound thoughts in his mind. He stared at her and slowly cocked his head to one side and brought his knife down to her blouse and fingered her buttons with the tip of the knife. One by one, he cut the buttons off her blows with the knife. She thought about taking another swing at his face, but the tip of his knife was now resting on her flesh right above her heart. He slowly moved it up towards her neck and cut her bra in half. He looked down at her breasts and her dark nipples and slowly moved his hand towards her left breast. When he touched her, she began to fight him with all her might. Her arms swung wild and her legs bucked underneath him like a wild horse.

"Agh! You swine!" He swore at her as she scratched his face again. He threw his head back and stabbed his knife in her side and twisted it into her kidney, puncturing and tearing it from its renal artery. Filled with rage, he pulled the knife out and stabbed her in her chest again and again and again and again. When he finally stopped to catch his breath, she was as limp as a fresh cadaver hanging from a branch. He looked down at her lying underneath him with her wide white eyes and gaping mouth staring back at him.

Terrified, he stood up and quickly and stared at himself covered in her blood. He began to panic. He quickly put his hands into his pocket and pulled out his pills. He looked at them and counted them. Hoping that he had counted wrong, he counted them again. What has he done? What day was it? He looked at his watch and saw that it was 4:30 in the afternoon. How long had he been waiting there? Two days? Three, maybe?

With his shaking sticky bloody hand, he popped one pill into his mouth and swallowed hard and its bitterness dried up the back of his throat. What was he going to tell his wife? He couldn't embarrass his family like this. He only meant to come in and talk to her and scare her a little. He didn't want to kill her. He didn't mean to kill her. What was he going to do now? Where was he going to hide the body?

He began pacing up and down the room holding his head in his hands. He looked out the window and knew he couldn't run away. He was in their territory and if they saw him, they would skin him alive on sight. He had done it and there was no turning back now.

He reached into his pocket again and popped another pill into his mouth. What difference was it going to make now? Angry with himself, he threw them across the room and continued pacing. As his blood began to boil, his mind was inundated with voices in his head. Why do they keep talking to him? What are they saying to him? Why are they screaming at him?

He fell to the floor and rummaged for the pills. He grabbed two and chewed them and swallowed them as quickly as possible. The voices didn't stop. They only became louder and louder. They didn't want to go away. They weren't going to leave him alone. He then reached for the gun in his holster and put it in his mouth and pulled the trigger.

Chapter Nine

January 15, 1979

Dear Maria,

I have finally got myself settled in and I am trying to live my life as an English man. I saw Charlie off atthe airport today and he couldn't wait to come home. War or no war, he was coming home, were his words.

Mama is doing fine. Charlie found her a home where she will be cared for every day. I visit herevery day and I try to remind her of Mtesa. I wish I hadpictures to show her, but all we have are memories.

Every day I watch the news and read the papersand try to keep in touch with what is going on in Graceland. I hear that Joseph Maleke has taken the stand to run theAfrican Democratic Movement Party. They say that heis Ted Tembo's successor. Is he as good of a speaker asthe great Tembo? I know how much you don't likepolitics, but maybe this man will bring an end to themassacres and violence in the country. The soonersomething is done, the sooner I can come home.I want you to know that I am thinking of youevery day and how much I still love you. Although I maybe thousands of miles away, you will always be a part of me.

Love you always,
Gulu

February 3, 1979

Dear Gulu,

I got your letter today and I was happy to hear from you. My mother found the letters you have been sending mesince you left and she inquired about you. I couldn't lie. I told her the truth. As you well know, I am not very good withwords and I regret not saying what I should have said to youa long time ago. Kungulu Zulu, I love you with all my heartand I always will. I want you to know that you were my firstlove and I will never forget you. When I told my mother this, she went and told my father. Without hesitation, he threw me out of the house. I didn't know what to do, so I called Charlie just as you had told me to do if I ever needed help. He really is awonderful man. He gave me a place to stay and a job as acashier at a supermarket. He took me to see Catherine andwe had a wonderful time. Wish you were here.

While we were away, there was a massacre at one ofthe coloured schools. The police officers were shooting leftand right killing school children. They say that what startedit was a black school boy who was refusing to be arrested.Then his friend, a white boy, tried to stick up for him. The police shot and killed both boys for not only refusing arrest, but for also attacking a police officer. It is really bad now, Gulu. It has turned out to be a blood bath between the people and the government. Now that they have started killing us all, black and white, what next?

I just hope that things will get better soon. I miss youvery much. I must go now. I have to be at work in fifteenminutes. I hope to hear from you soon.

With love always, Maria

October 10, 1980

Dear Maria,

University life is really something here. I find myself having sleepless nights and endless work. Nowthat I am in Oxford, I cannot see mama every day. I goto London every weekend and try to spend as much timewith her as I can before driving back to Oxford.While I was in a pub with some friends inLondon, I met a boy from Mtesa. He is a white boyabout my age and his family left after the school childrenmassacre. He told me that his younger brother died inthat massacre. His parents vowed not to return until thepeople of Graceland learned to live in peace. As far as he isconcerned, he has no country. Tony and I have become good friends. He is the first white Mtesa friend, otherthan you, that I have ever had. I don't think we wouldhave ever met (let alone become friends) if we werehome.

It is starting to rain again. I have never seen somuch rain in a country. I will write to you soon.

Love,
Gulu

February 14, 1982

Dear Gulu,

It is Valentine's Day and I have nobody to spend it with. All I have been doing all day is think about youand the good times we had. I was reading through allthe letters you sent me and I felt like you were right herewith me telling me your stories. Your letters havealready filled my little box and I need to find another tostore your new ones. Four years of letters can reallypile up.

I saw mother today. I was walking by a clothingstore and when I looked in; I saw her trying on a dresswith a friend. She didn't see me. She looked so happyand beautiful. I wanted to go in and speak to her, but Ididn't want to spoil her moment so I walked on to work.I wish things were different. At least I have yourletters to keep me going.

Missing you dearly,
Maria

May 30, 1982

Dear Maria,

I graduate today. Everybody's family is here to see them receive their diploma except for me. Mama isnot doing too well and she is now bed ridden. Tony andhis family came to my graduation though. They have been very good to me. Tony's father has offered me ajob as a reporter for his magazine 'Politics Today.' Hewants me to feature African politics, something that Iknow very well and comes easy to me. My first piecewill be on the evolution of Graceland to its independence in 1980 as Mtesa. I could write that with my eyes closed.

When I went to tell mama about the good news, she was not doing very well. Ever since she fell into acoma last week, the doctors don't think her condition isgoing to change any time soon. Seeing her live by amachine is really difficult for me to accept. I can't standseeing her like this anymore. Maria, I have never beenso scared and so alone in my life.

I have to go. I promise to write more next time.

Love,
Gulu

January 17, 1983

Dear Gulu,

I wish I could be there for you right now. I am sure it is not easy dealing with your mother's death alone. The most difficult thing for me was to tell Charlie. He didn't take it very well. He locked himselfup in his room and drank all day. I didn't know that him and your mother were lovers. He couldn't stop talkingabout her until I nursed him back to be sober.

I hope you will be coming home soon, because Idon't want to see myself grieving over you like the wayCharlie has done over your mother. Please, come homesoon. Charlie and I need you.

Miss you,
Maria

December 1, 1984

Dear Maria,

I told Tony's father that I would not be renewing my twoyear contract because I was returning home. It was noteasy, but I did it anyway. The more I thought about you, the more there was a reason for me to come home. Ithas been four years since our independence, and I amfour years over due to return.
I can't wait to see you.

Lots of love,
Gulu

Chapter Ten
1985

He stepped up to the counter and handed his passport to the white man sitting behind the counter. His heart started to beat more rapidly when he watched the man scribble on a piece of paper and then in his passport. He flinched when the man stamped his passport with a loud bang! With a casual smile, the man handed the passport back to him and said,

"Welcome to Mtesa, Mr Zulu. I hope your stay will be a pleasant one." Kungulu felt kind of odd being treated like that. None the less, he forced a smile on his face and kindly replied,

"Thank you."

He went through customs and like a tourist, he watched the people around him bustle earnestly. He watched a white woman embrace a black man and passionately kiss him. That was a normal sight in London, but he never expected to see anything like that in Mtesa. He looked around him to see if anyone else was watching them and whether anyone was going to react to their public display of affection, but nobody seemed to care. He walked out into the street struggling with his luggage and attracted three taxi drivers who were eager to help him. He settled for the older gentleman who gladly offered to take him on a tour of one of the most renowned metropolitan cities of Africa.

"Maybe some other time. Could you take me to the Holiday Inn?"

"Yes sir." The driver detected an accent in his passenger's voice. "If you don't mind me asking, where are you from, sir?"

"I am from here, Mtesa."

"Then why a hotel? Don't you have family?"

"No." He answered regretfully. "My only family died two years ago."

"So sorry, sir."

"That's all right. I just wished I could have buried her here, in her homeland." He sadly looked out his window into the city which was filled with high rises and noisy traffic, sidewalks scattered with men and women in suits rushing to and from work. "I have been gone too long." He said to himself.

"Sorry, sir?" The driver asked thinking he was talking to him.

"I said I have been gone too long."

"For how long, sir?"

"I left the day Ted Tembo was shot."

"Oh sir, a lot has happened since then, especially after our independence."

"I know." He said quietly. "I wish I could have been here."

"Sir, no. It was horrible, too many people died through the struggle. You are still young. It is good you come back now. Some people like you don't come back. They forget where they come from, no? My friend, let me show you something. It is something all people of Mtesa should see and be reminded of everyday. I will not charge you for the fare."

"Okay, and then from there I go straight to the hotel."

"Yes sir."

"Please, call me Kungulu."

217

"Okay, Kungulu." The driver smiled at him through his rear view mirror and spun the car around into the next street.

Gulu watched the city as his tour guide drove through the traffic. The taxi finally stopped in a park. It was the same park he remembered being divided in two. One side was for blacks and the other for the whites. Now both types of people walked freely from one side to the other. In the middle of the park was a tall bronze statue of a weeping woman holding a dead child in her arms, while another child clung to her side crying and sucking on two fingers. This was the statue of "Weeping Mama Africa," and at the base of her feet it said, 'Children of Africa are dying. Stop the violence and you will save our future.'

Below the inscription where flowers were laid, were the lists of children's names, both black and white, and their ages, who died during the struggle. The long list trailed back the day Ted Tembo died until Independence Day on October 5, 1980. The list seemed to be endless.

"You see, if you didn't leave, you could have been on that list, my friend. Not even all the children's names are on their. Too many died and too many suffered," said the taxi driver. Kungulu knelt down and fingered the engraved names and remembered the police interrogations, the riots, the tear gas, the gun shots....He bowed his head and quietly remembered.

"Please, take me to my hotel." He said hoarsely. He cleared his throat and swallowed hard, pushing the pain far down deep inside of him. When Kungulu got to the hotel and checked in, he made one call and in twenty minutes, the front desk called him to tell him that his guests were waiting for him in the lounge. Feeling the butterflies flutter in his stomach, he took the elevator down to the lobby and when he stepped out of the elevator, Catherine ran towards him and threw her arms around him and began to cry with joy.

"Now, why would you have to go and do that for? Blubbering all over me, are you?" Kungulu fought back his own tears and dried hers with his thumbs. He greeted Munique with a hug and heavy hand shake and then looked down at their twin girls.

"My God, Catherine, they are beautiful. He took them both in his arms and hugged them tightly. The seven year old girls felt awkward being hugged by a stranger, but they politely smiled and blushed equally.

"Hello, Gulu." Maria's soft voice got his attention. He looked up and remembered her just as he had last seen her. Her smile was as genuine as her sparkling eyes. He cupped her face in his hands and kissed her tenderly. "It's good to have you back, Gulu," she said. They hugged tightly and he whispered in her ear

"I swear, this time, I am never going to let you go." When they looked deep into each other's eyes, a child tugged at her dress.

"Oh, sorry my love." She smiled at the child and then Gulu was lost for words. He looked down at the little boy with large dark wondrous eyes with fine light brown curls. He knelt down and looked at the boy at eye level and smiled.

"Hello and what is your name?" The child hesitated to answer and looked up at his mother. She nodded at him and in a small voice he said,

"Kungulu."

Caught by surprise, Kungulu's eyes were fixated on the child. He then was able to find his voice again. "That is a nice name. At least it is better than David Coolbear, don't you think?" He stood up and looked at Maria and searched her face for an answer.

219

"I.....I wanted to tell you, but I didn't know how. Each time I wrote I...." She waited for his reaction because now she was lost for words. She watched him smile at his own son. He lifted him up and hugged him and when little Kungulu hugged him back, Gulu sighed with joy. Little Kungulu was happy to finally meet his father, the person who his mother always talked about and always promised that one day he was going to come home to them. With little Kungulu still in his arms, he looked over at Maria.

"Don't try to explain, Maria." He touched her face tenderly and gently added, "I have a son and you, that's all that matters now."

"Then you're not mad at me?"

"Mad at you? No. Maybe disappointed that you didn't tell me sooner, but not mad." He kissed her on the forehead and she smile with relief. "I have a son!" He whispered happily. Everyone was happy to see his acceptance of his son and there was a repetition of hugs and kisses amongst all of them.

"Well, all this love in the air is making me hungry." proclaimed Munique. "How about some lunch? I am starving." They started to walk out of the hotel and Gulu asked,

"Where is Charlie?"

"He is trying to find a parking space outside. He can't wait to see you. He was upset that you checked into the hotel before checking with us." Said Catherine.

"I guess I will have to check out sometime today, don't I?"

"I don't think you have much of a choice." She laughed and they all walked out of the hotel together.

EPILOGUE

Just as he was closing the book, the captain announced that they were going to be landing in fifteen minutes. Matthew looked out his window and hoped his mother would not see him get emotional over the book.

"Are you all right?" She asked. It was too latenow. She had already seen him. He batted his eyes to wipe away the tears that almost trailed from his long lashes. He turned to her and unexpectedly found himself asking her,

"Why didn't you tell me?" She looked at him and knew exactly what he was referring to. She did not know how to answer. She opened her mouth to speak, but she did not know what to say. She kept quiet and felt guilty about not telling him sooner about his own people and his own family. "I had the right to know what kind of man my father was, mum. I had the right to know. If you never married him, why do you still keep his name?" He could not hold his emotions in any longer and uncontrollably, the tears he tried to bat away, now flowed endlessly down his face to the tip of his chin. He turned away again and looked out the window at the misty clouds and through them, appeared Africa.

When they had finally landed and had checked themselves through customs, Matthew felt like he had been there and was going through the motions he had once done before. He could feel the butterflies in his stomach as he remembered the last chapter of the book he was reading. They climbed into the taxi and as they were driving away, Matthew held the book in his lap and stared at the cover. He turned to his mother and said, "Mum, can we go see the statue of MamaAfrica in the park?" She looked at him and could see that he was beginning to understand why she brought him back home. She smiled at him and took his hand in hers and squeezed it without saying a word. She leaned forward and asked the taxi driver to take themto the park where the statue of Mama Africa was. The taxi driver agreed and smiled to his passengersthrough his rear view mirror.

"First time to Mtesa" He asked.

"No, we are returning home." She replied.

"Yes, every person from Mtesa should never forget Mama Africa. She gave us our freedom." Said the old taxi driver. "I was here, during the struggle...." The taxi driver began to tell his story, but Matthew was not listening anymore. He was too lost in his thoughts. He was not quite sure whether it was pain or hate or joy he was feeling. He just hadthe need to go see the statue for himself.

When they arrived at the park, he lost himself in Kungulu's steps and motions when he saw the statue of Mama Africa. He knelt down at the foot of the statue and fingered the many names of the children who had died during the struggle. He wished he understood why and how his own people's history had to be that way. Without realising how much his emotions had taken over him, tears streamed down his face and remembered Kungulu's experiences in the book. His mother knelt down beside him and put her arm around him and also shared his sorrow.

"This could have been me, mum. My name could have been on here with all the other children...." he

223

thought about his reckless lifestyle and said, I should be on here instead of these children."

"No, Matthew. Nobody's child deserves to be on this list." His mother began to reassure him. "I left only because I wanted a better life for you ....so your name would not end up at the feet of Mama Africa."

Quietly, they mourned the loss of their own people and Mrs Belmont was happy to see that her son understood the importance of their return home. She cleared her throat and wiped her tears away with her white handkerchief and said, "Let's go. It's timefor you to meet your father." Before they left, they stared into the eyes of Mama Africa and the children that clung to her side. It all seemed to come together. Everything seemed to make sense now and a sense of relief came over them.

They got back into the taxi and drove through the busy traffic until they arrived in the quietsuburbs. The taxi pulled up at house numbernineteen with a large white electronic gate. The taxidriver helped them with their bags and Matthew's mother paid the fare. Nervously, she rang the doorbell and took a deep breath to clear her mind. Two large Dobermans ran to the gate and viciouslybarked showing their sharp off-white fangs at them. A man came out of the house and walked towards thegate in long strides. He called his dogs and orderedthem to heal. Obediently, they obeyed their masterand parked themselves to the side of the gate. The electronic gate automatically slid open and in mid step, he stopped. He stared at the woman and the boy standing next to her. Remembering his manners, he approached them and with a nervous smile he said,

"I called the airport and they told me that youwere arriving at seven this evening."

"There were two flights. We came in on the afternoon flight." She tried to smile, but her nerves took over her expression. Matthew stared at the man and could not take his eyes off him. The man reached for their bags and showed them to the house. He put the bags in the middle of the living room and quickly started tidying up the loose pages of the newspaper that were lying on the floor and on the couch. "Excuse the mess." He said. He then remembered his manners and stopped what he was doing and stared at the two of them. He reached out his hand to Matthew and without blinking he said,

"You must be Matthew." Matthew shook his hand and said nothing. "Your mother wrote to me about you...." He didn't know what else to say. Matthew just stared at him. The man diverted his eyes from Matthew and turned to his mother. "Did you have a good flight?" he asked as he nervously scratched the back of his head.

"It was fine." Matthew answered for her.
They both looked at him and continued staring at this stranger who was his father.

"You must be very tired." The man finally said. "Let me show you to your rooms." He picked up their bags again and showed her to her room and then Matthew to his room. Before he left Matthew alone, he said,

"Matthew, I am glad your mother told me about you. I just wish she would have told me sooner." Matthew did not look at him. He sat on the bed and looked out his bedroom window. Not knowing what else to say, he left him alone and closed the door behind him.

He went into the next room to see her. She was unpacking when he walked in. When she saw

225

him, she stopped unpacking and turned her attention to him.

"I am glad you brought him here." There was a moment of silence between them. "Why didn't you tell me earlier?"

"Because, it wouldn't have made a difference. Back then you were so absorbed in yourself.....feeling sorry for yourself."

"Yes, but I had the right to know."
She did not know what to say to that. Once again, there was a moment of silence between them.

"He's got your eyes." She said softly.

"Dinner will be ready in half an hour." He said, and walked out.

Half an hour later, Charlie knocked onMatthew's door.

"Dinner's ready." He said through the door.

"I'm not hungry." Came the response. He quietly walked away and went to Mary's room. Her door was slightly open and when he looked in, she had fallen asleep on the bed fully dressed with her shoes still on. He quietly walked in and took a blanket out of the cupboard and quietly covered her. He stared at her and realised how time had flown. He closed the door behind him and went outside to smoke a cigarette. He lit his cigarette and sat back in his lawn chair. He inhaled deeply and blew the smoke above his head and watched it disappear in the atmosphere. He looked up into the sky and watched the auburn residue of the sun's shadow disappear behind the houses and building of the city as it was pushed out of sight by the indigo night sky. Slowly, the stars started to appear with the drifting night. Matthew crept out of the house and at adistance, he watched the man who was his, quietlysitting and watching the night blanket the country.

As the night fell over the city, his father was lowly transformed into a silhouette. He stared at his longlegs stretched out in front of him in his old tattered jeans and cotton shirt... He watched him put his hands through his hair and the long strands fell back in their place over his eye. He was in his own sanctuary, inhaling and exhaling the smoke and watched it trail above him. What did his mother and all the other women see in this man? Matthew stepped up closer and eventually caught Charlie's attention.

"Can I have a smoke?" Surprised, Charlie gave him one and before he lit it, he asked,

"Does you mother know you smoke?"

"I won't tell if you won't." Said Matthew. Charlie smiled and gave him a light to light his cigarette. He pulled up a chair for him and they both languidly sat in his yard and smoked their cigarettes languidly.

"Did your mother ever tell you about the African skies?"

"No." Matthew lied.

"All Africans, black and white should know about our African skies. Our skies never lie. They are always telling the truth. You see, many, many, years ago, when our forefathers, meaning yours and mine, always used the sky for guidance." Matthew kept his eyes fixed on the winking stars, and listened to his father's voice. He had dreamed of this day for a long time and for a long time, he had convinced himself that it was all just a dream. He would have never thought that he would actually be having a savouring moment with his father as they sat underneath the African skies listening to him tell him about old legendary stories about his people. Wide eyed, he saw the clear bright stars dancing in the clear night. "Whether the sun was up or the moon was full, it had a meaning," Charlie continued, "sometimes

227

they predicted wars and sometimes they predicted peace. Sometimes even love if you looked hard enough at the stars. Like tonight, for example. The moon is full; the stars are shining.....that is telling us that everything is in sequence. It is going in a steady flow. If you are in love, you will see your lover's face in the moon. But if there is lightning, thunder and heavy storms, something terrible is supposed to happen. Maybe death, war, destruction..." He looked over at Matthew and he was fast asleep. He got up and got a blanket to cover him. Just as he covered him, he stared at Matthew and felt a warm feeling go through him. He wanted to lean in close and hold him against him and protect him. Instead, he let him sleep soundly in the chair and he sat down in his chair and also dozed off and for the first time in a long time, he slept without a worry in his mind.

The End